The
Journey Home

Other Apple Paperbacks
you might enjoy:

Risk N' Roses
by Jan Slepian

Thirteen Never Changes
by Budge Wilson

Why the Whales Came
by Michael Morpurgo

Kate's House
Mary Francis Shura

Kate's Book
Mary Francis Shura

The Journey Home

Isabelle Holland

AN
APPLE
PAPERBACK

SCHOLASTIC INC.
New York Toronto London Auckland Sydney

ISBN 0-590-43111-0

Copyright © 1990 by Isabelle Holland.
All rights reserved. Published by Scholastic Inc.
APPLE PAPERBACKS® is a registered trademark of Scholastic Inc.

12 11 10 9 8 7 6 5 4 3 2   4 5 6 7 8/9

Printed in the U.S.A.   28

*To Eunice Blake Bohanon
with appreciation*

I would like to express my appreciation to the Children's Aid Society of New York for their cooperation and help when I was doing the research for *The Journey Home*.

The Journey Home

One

There was the sound of steps coming up the creaking stairs of the tenement followed by a knock on the door.

The three inside froze. Mrs. Lavin hadn't been able to pay rent for two months, ever since her illness had become suddenly worse.

"Quiet!" she hissed now to her two daughters, holding Annie's head against her shoulder and reaching out to grip Maggie's hand. All three fixedly stared at the door.

The knock sounded again. "Are there any sick children in there?"

Mrs. Lavin, who had been holding her breath, let it out now, and then coughed. "Come in."

The door opened. A young man with thick

fair hair and gray eyes came in, carrying a doctor's bag.

"Annie, me darlin'," Mrs. Lavin said. "Be taking the chamber pot down to the privy for me. There's a luv!"

A stubborn look came over seven-year-old Annie's face. "It's Maggie's turn. I took it down last time."

"Well, Maggie'll do it next."

Annie's underlip went out. "I don't — "

"Ach! Do it! Be gone with you!"

Stamping her boots, Annie did as she'd been told. The doctor stepped aside for her. "Are either of your children sick, ma'am?" he asked politely.

For a moment Maggie imagined him holding his breath against the stench of the room, indeed, of the whole tenement house. The thought was galling to her pride, which, as the nuns and the priest in confession were fond of pointing out, was her greatest sin.

"Are either — ?" the doctor began again.

"No, but I am," Mrs. Lavin said. "I'll soon be dead, and I want to know from you exactly how I can arrange to have my girls sent on one of the orphan trains west."

"Ma! No!" Maggie almost shouted.

"Hush now!" her mother ordered.

"I'll not go!"

2

"You'll do as you're told! The both of you!"

The doctor put down his bag and came over to the bed. "The Children's Aid Society . . ." he began.

Twenty minutes later he was telling Mrs. Lavin and Maggie where the children were to go and whom to ask for. "It's a Miss Trent," he said, "at the lodging on Greene Street." He had also agreed to make arrangements to have Mrs. Lavin taken to Bellevue Hospital. "And you will be told exactly where the children are so that you can keep in touch with them."

"I won't be here long enough to do that. All I want is that they should get out of this city of the Devil. I don't have to tell you what can happen to two girls, do I?"

"No." He got up. "I'll send the ambulance. Just give them this note. And here's a note your daughters can give to Miss Trent at the lodging house." He scribbled on a pad and handed Mrs. Lavin a second piece of paper. "They're in good health, I take it?" he said, smiling a little.

"Aye. They're fine. And I want them to stay that way."

Maggie listened to the doctor's steps going rapidly down the filthy, rickety stairs.

When she turned back she looked down at

her mother lying in the bed, at the face that was almost as gray as the gray in her hair above. It was often hard for Maggie to remember that her mother was barely thirty-one, and that thirty-one was not considered old by many people. Her brown hair had started going gray when Da had died three years before.

For a moment, looking down at her mother, Maggie saw instead her father as she had last seen him the morning before he died. Tall, with Maggie's dark hair and gray eyes, he, too, looked older than his twenty-nine years. But Maggie could remember him, full of the wayward charm that Annie had inherited, standing with her on the dock in Liverpool, waiting to board the ship that would bring them to the New World, his face so full of light and enthusiasm that six-year-old Maggie had felt infused and warmed by its hope.

In the grim years that followed, that hope slowly died. There was work to be had, but it was infrequent and poorly paid. Michael Lavin, volatile and easily discouraged, came slowly to spend more time in the Green Harp and other saloons. And when his wife, struggling to feed two children, and with the beginnings of the disease that wasted her, rebuked him, he told her shortly that the saloons were where Irishmen of influence gathered, and they'd soon have a better job for him. Then, one day, after he'd spent more time than he should have at the bar, he'd moved carelessly on the ship where he was working and been hit and instantly killed by the boom.

"Maggie!"

"Yes, Ma?" She bent over her mother, seeing the sheen that lay over her skin. The room was chilly, yet her mother was sweating around her face and head. "Are you too hot, Ma?"

"No, Maggie. It's just the fever."

Maggie went over to a bowl on a table near the window to wet a rag to use as a compress on her mother's forehead.

As Maggie was bathing her mother's face, Mrs. Lavin suddenly caught her hand. "As soon as I've gone to the hospital, you and Annie go to the Aid Society's lodging and be giving the paper the doctor left to the lady there, the one he mentioned."

"Ma, I'm not going to leave you. And that's that." Maggie went back to the bowl to rinse out the greasy cloth. She heard the bed creak and turned to see her mother trying to lean forward.

"Ye'll do as I say!" The words came out with so much energy that her mother started coughing.

Maggie ran back to the bed, saw the froth

on her mother's mouth, and dived under the bed for the slop jar.

Several minutes later Mrs. Lavin lay back, her face wet, her mouth spattered with blood. One hand was pressed against her chest. With the other she was holding onto Maggie's hand. They were both quiet for a while. Maggie replaced the jar under the bed, then pressed the wet cloth from the bowl over her mother's forehead and mouth. "Ma," she whispered. "Ma. You'll be all right. Father O'Mara says to make another novena on Friday."

"No novena's going to get the muck out of my lungs." The words came out with bitterness.

"Don't you believe in miracles, Ma?"

Mrs. Lavin opened her eyes again and looked at her older daughter. "I do," she said. "But the ways of God are mysterious. I've been thinking, lying here all this time. Maybe it's God's way of sending you west, out of the filth and the slum."

"He wouldn't do that to you just to send Annie and me on the train," Maggie said angrily.

"Sure, now, Mag, you don't know what He'd be doing. Didn't He make heaven and earth? It's not for us to be asking for explanations." She paused, her chest rising and falling as she fought for breath. Then, "Maggie, I want you and Annie to get on that train. The Aid Society says there are people out west who want children and will treat them right."

"We're not going to leave you, Ma."

"I have the sickness, Mag. And it won't be long now. You know how the prayer asks for a happy death. I want that, Mag. I want to know that you and Annie will be going to where ye'll have a change, away from these streets of hell." Suddenly she caught Maggie's hand. "Promise me, Maggie. Promise me!"

"But . . . but we'll never see you again."

"We'll meet at the feet of the Blessed Virgin herself, and I'll be asking her to look out for you, every moment."

Maggie, sitting on the bed, stared down at the stained blanket. "Father O'Mara — "

"Father O'Mara is a man. What he knows is the Church! He's not a mother!"

They were both quiet. Mrs. Lavin tried to catch her breath, while Maggie stared at the blanket. Maggie knew that, along with other Catholic priests, Father O'Mara bitterly resented the work of the Reverend Charles Loring Brace of the Children's Aid Society, which picked homeless children off the street and sent them with a guardian on the boat to Albany, and then on trains west where some of the settlers and farmers were eager to adopt the children.

"I don't want to leave you," Maggie said stubbornly. Then her eyes filled, and she began to cry.

"Ye'll be fine out there," Mrs. Lavin said. "I've heard the air is clean out west, and there are decent people. I've seen what happens here to girls who are left without parents. I'll not have that happen to you and Annie." She made a movement with her hand. "Tell me it won't, Mag!"

"Ma — "

"Promise me, Mag!"

Maggie nodded and then wiped the tears from her face. "I promise," she said.

They both knew what Mrs. Lavin was talking about. Girls as young as twelve, no older than Maggie, were walking the streets as prostitutes.

As she spoke the door opened, and Annie came in with the empty chamber pot that she thrust under the bed.

Mrs. Lavin put out a thin hand and touched the rough woolen jacket, obviously a man's, with its sleeves folded far back and its bottom edge almost sweeping the floor. "Where'd you be getting the coat, luv?" she asked.

"Mrs. O'Gorman at the Green Harp gave it to me for looking after Timmie. She said it belonged to Mr. O'Gorman who dropped dead."

Mrs. Lavin pulled herself up a little. In her

gray face her blue eyes were startlingly like Annie's.

"Ye'll not be hanging around that saloon, now," she said. "And yer covered with dog hairs. Fleas, no doubt, too!"

"Timmie doesn't have fleas. He's a good dog." She came to the end of the bed. Her wide mouth broke into a sunny smile. "How're yer feeling, Ma? Did the doctor make you better?"

"He will. But I don't want you around that tavern. Drink! It was the cause of your father's death!"

"I thought a boom on a ship killed him," Maggie said.

Mrs. Lavin narrowed her lips. "Aye. It did. But he'd been to the Green Harp before he went onto the docks and wasn't watching his way." Another fit of coughing seized her.

"Ma!" A cry broke from Annie, and she hurled herself across the bed towards her mother.

"No — stay away from me! It's not — Now, don't cry, Annie! It just makes things worse! Go now!" But Mrs. Lavin's arm went around Annie and, almost as though against her will, she hugged her child to her and rocked back and forth. "And we must be talking about the train west that you and Maggie will be taking."

And then as Annie's face crumbled, "Now Annie, you know that I want you to go!"

"No!" Annie cried. "I don't want to go! And anyway, Father O'Mara says they'll all be making us Protestants."

Mrs. Lavin pressed Annie against her shoulder, and rubbed her back. "No one can force you to be anything you don't want now, Annie."

"Father O'Mara says that they won't let the children eat until they promise to stop being Catholics and be Protestants and to say that the Pope is an evil man and there's no Blessed Mother and — "

"Hush now! That's enough! They're nothing but stories made up by the likes of Mrs. O'Gorman, standing as she is behind the bar all night with nothing to do but pour beer and talk to the drinking men. I'll not have you believing her and passing on her stories."

"But Father O'Mara — "

"If Father O'Mara is that keen on your being such good Catholics, then let him find some good Catholic home for you. It's all very well for the Church to be forbidding this and forbidding that, but then let it find something of its own! And while we're talking on the subject, have you been to First Communion class with Sister Catherine?"

"I forgot." Annie pulled away from her mother and giggled.

"You told me you were going yesterday," Maggie said.

"I forgot . . . Timmie . . . Mrs. O'Gorman . . ." She looked from Maggie to her mother. "I forgot," she said a third time and lowered her eyes. Catching sight of the slop jar, she said quickly, "I can take that to the privy, too." She scrambled off the bed and clasped the handle of the jar. She added virtuously, "Even though it's twice Maggie's turn."

"And what if Timmie should suddenly run in?" Maggie asked. "What would happen to the jar then?" But she was smiling in spite of herself. With her yellow hair every which way Annie looked almost like a dirty angel with a halo.

"She'll empty it properly now, won't you, Annie?" Mrs. Lavin said.

Annie gave her gap-toothed smile. "Yes."

After she'd gone Mrs. Lavin lay back against her pillow. Her cheeks were flushed. The nightgown beneath her shawl rose and fell. She said finally, "Ye'll have to be patient with her, Maggie." Then stopped as she coughed and wheezed for a few seconds. "She's not like you."

Maggie sighed. "When there's work to be done she sits there and makes up stories or plays with Timmie or sings him little songs. I know I shouldn't shout at her. But — Sister Catherine says she has a head full of pictures."

"She does that. Ye can't help it and neither can she. Ye'll have to be patient." Mrs. Lavin hesitated a moment. "She's like her da, that is, before the drink took him."

The door opened, and Annie came in, swinging the slop jar by the handle.

"Thank you, luv," Mrs. Lavin said.

"There's a great big beautiful dog at the bottom of the yard," Annie said dreamily as she pushed the jar under the bed.

Mrs. Lavin gave a sharp look. "And who does it belong to? There are no dogs in this house, I'm happy to say."

"He said he was looking for a home, and — "

"That's — " Maggie broke out, and then stopped as her mother tugged on her hand. "Now you know you just made that up, Annie, didn't you?"

"But it could be true, don't you think?" Annie said pleadingly. Then she grinned and skipped to the door.

The men from Bellevue arrived the next day and carried Mrs. Lavin down the steep, dirty stairs to their ambulance.

Maggie stood on the street, holding Annie's

hand, watching the men slide her mother's slight form into the wagon.

"Ma!" Annie yelled, tugging at the hand that held her. "Ma — don't go. We'll take care of you. Mag — don't let them take her away!"

"Annie, I told you. They're going to give her medicine and take good care of her. Better than we can. Now I told you that!"

"No, no!" But Annie stopped trying to pull her hand away. She stood there, crying.

"Where're they taking her?" A woman standing by the steps asked. Other women and children had gathered.

"We're taking her to Bellevue," one of the medical attendants said.

"That'll be the end of her," another voice spoke up from the back of the little crowd.

"No," Maggie said. It was what Mrs. Lavin herself had said, and part of Maggie knew it was true. But she fiercely rejected it. No matter what her mother had said, Maggie wanted to believe that by some miracle her mother would be well, and they would all be together where there was clean air and decent people. "No," she said. "Ma's going to be fine. They'll give her medicine and then she'll be all right and can come and be with us."

"Ma!" Annie cried. "Ma, don't go. Please don't go."

Taking advantage of Maggie's momentary

inattention, she snatched her hand free and flung herself at the ambulance, trying to scramble inside.

One of the men who was settling Mrs. Lavin came to the edge of the ambulance. "You can't come with her. She'll be all right. Later, maybe, if your doctor says it is all right, you'll come and see her. Now give over! Stop that!"

By this time Annie was half inside the ambulance, but Maggie got hold of her and pulled her out and onto the street.

"I'm going with her," Annie yelled. "Leave me be!"

But Maggie held her fast. The ambulance doors closed. The driver flicked his whip, yelled "Giddyap" to the horses, and they trotted off.

Annie stood in the middle of the street and howled, her hands over her face, tears dropping down beneath them.

"Annie," Maggie said quietly. "Stop that now!"

"Ma's going to die," Annie sobbed. "She's going to die, and you're going to let her!"

"Be quiet!" Maggie said, angry because she knew she was near to breaking into sobs herself, because behind her determination to do what Ma had wanted hovered despair. The women around were looking at them, and Maggie wondered if they, too, were condemning her. It was true; nobody from the street or the neighborhood had ever come back from Bellevue.

"If you're rich," one of the women said, "they'll make you better. But if you're Irish and poor you die."

Maggie whirled around. "You're not to say that!"

The woman shrugged and moved off.

"And what's going to happen to you and Annie?" another woman said.

"We're going west, on the train for orphans," Maggie replied. And then, stubbornly, "It's what Ma wants for us."

"And what will Father O'Mara be saying about that? It's well known it's just a way for the Protestants to convert good Catholic children."

"Ma said we don't have to be anything we don't want to be. Come on, Annie. We have to get to the lodging house."

Two

The lodging house run by the Children's Aid Society was on a narrow street not far from the docks. The building was a low brick hall that looked dirty and run-down. The door was open, and children stood around the steps talking. When Maggie and Annie walked up, they stopped.

"Have you come for the trains?" one boy, who looked about eleven, asked. The trousers and jacket he wore were patched and far too large for him, but they looked clean and warm.

"Yes," Maggie said. She glanced at the piece of paper the young doctor had given Mrs. Lavin. It was easy to read the address, because she could read numbers, and he had mentioned the name of the street. But though the nuns had taught her some letters, Maggie couldn't really read anything else. Like many of the children in the neighborhood she hadn't spent much time in school. She'd been too busy looking after Annie when Ma and Da were at work, and then later, when Ma got sick, looking after her as well and making what money she could selling matches and running errands. Nevertheless, Maggie was bitterly ashamed of her inability to read and didn't like to admit it.

She pretended to peer at the paper. "There's a lady we have to see."

"Miss Trent?"

"Yes," Maggie said. "That's the name."

"She's inside," the boy said. Then, "What's your name?"

"Maggie. And this is my sister, Annie."

"Hullo. Mine's Lawrence. Miss Trent said somebody might adopt me even though I'm lame."

Maggie glanced down and saw that one of his legs was shorter than the other. "I'm sure they will," she said quickly.

At that moment a tall young woman appeared in the doorway, saw them, and stopped. "Are you looking for me?"

Looking up at her, Maggie felt a familiar jab of wounded pride and resentment. Miss Trent was plain and her clothes severe, yet there was

17

something about her, perhaps the way she held herself, that took Maggie back to a chilly, rainy day when she and other children were trying to sell matches outside A.T. Stewart, the big department store on the corner of Broadway and Tenth Street, across from Grace Church. A carriage had drawn up. A lady stepped down onto the street. Maggie rushed forward holding up her matches. The haughty lady's face as she turned away from Maggie's hand now flooded Maggie's memory. There had been fur around the lady's cloak. She had had on gloves. A faint, sweet aroma had drifted across to Maggie, making her aware of the staleness of her own clothes and the foul smell from the gutter where she stood. More than anything else in Maggie's mind cleanness marked that other world, the world of the fur-covered ladies, of carriages and glossy horses and coachmen who looked at Maggie and the other street children as though they were dirt. The lady had disdained the matches Maggie had held out, but without looking at her had placed a dime in her hand.

And now this Miss Trent, standing above her on the steps of the lodging house, for all the fact that she didn't look rich or haughty, brought back the memory and the feeling.

Maggie swallowed. "Yes. The doctor said I

was to give you this." And Maggie walked up the steps and gave the woman the note that the doctor had given her.

The woman took it and smiled at her. Then she said, "Hello, Lawrence."

"Hello, Miss Trent."

She looked back at Maggie and Annie. "You're the sisters Dr. Purdy sent me a note about. He said that your mother . . . your mother was ill, and he'd made arrangements to have her taken to Bellevue."

"Yes," Maggie said. "Ma said you'd take us out west on the train."

"I will have to go and see her myself to make sure that's what she wants." The angular face lit up with a smile. "But I'm sure, from what the doctor said, it is."

Suddenly Annie said loudly, "I don't want to go. I don't want to leave Ma."

Maggie turned and took her hand. "It's what Ma wanted. She said that. You heard her."

"I won't go," Annie said.

Maggie tightened her hand on Annie's. "She'll be all right," she said to the young woman. "It's just the . . . the shock of it now."

"I'm sure it is." Miss Trent bent over Annie and said, "You know, you don't think so now, but you'll like it out west. The air is clean, and people are waiting to adopt you and give you a home, and you'll have grass and trees instead of these dirty streets." She looked down at Annie's face, streaked with tears and dirt. "It'll be so much easier to stay clean there. And we'll give you fresh, clean clothes to travel with."

The lady bountifuls, Ma had called them when she worked in their great houses, Maggie thought now. Always, as Ma had said, somehow making you feel dirtier than you already felt. They had given Ma clothes that their children had grown out of. Maggie knew she was supposed to be grateful, but hated wearing clothes other people had worn. Even when they were the only ones she had.

"I don't want to be clean," Annie said.

Miss Trent glanced at Maggie. "I hope you'll be able to . . . to make her see that going on the train is the best thing she could do. If she doesn't, that would mean that the two of you would have to go to an orphanage here in the city, or near it, and that wouldn't be anywhere near as nice."

"She'll be all right," Maggie said. She was starting to be afraid that if Annie went on like this the Children's Aid people wouldn't let them go on the train. "She'll be fine," she went on, as though the words themselves could make Annie change.

"I hope so," Miss Trent said, straightening.

"Go on in, now. Supper will be served soon. I'm sure you're hungry."

The next morning Maggie was helping with the clearing and washing up after breakfast when she suddenly realized that Annie was missing. She debated telling Miss Trent, who was in the kitchen organizing the washing up. But despite the kindness she sensed in the young woman, Maggie felt a basic mistrust of English-sounding Americans like Miss Trent. She wasn't stuck-up or proud the way so many of the people Ma had worked for had been. But Maggie couldn't get rid of her memory of what Ma had said about them: "They're so full of their own haughtiness they'd swallow themselves, if it weren't for their teeth."

Whenever Maggie recalled that, she remembered the lady stepping from the carriage, smelling of lavender, looking as though the dirt of the people in the street around her didn't exist. Part of Maggie resented her bitterly. Part of her wanted to be just like her.

And when she and Annie went west, she thought now, surreptitously drying her hands, they would learn how to look like that and smell like that and be like that. But for now she had to find Annie, and she wanted to do it without anyone realizing they were missing.

Quietly Maggie slipped out the back door, knowing that if Miss Trent saw her leave, she would assume Maggie was going to the privy at the back of the hall. The only problem might be if there were not a way to get back to the street from there, but Maggie thought she remembered a narrow alley that led from the outside to the street behind, and she could escape to look for Annie without anyone knowing.

Once on the street, Maggie turned her steps north and east to the old neighborhood where the streets were meaner and the waterfront full of taverns and shops and brothels. Partly running and partly walking, Maggie finally caught up with Annie, trudging towards the Green Harp.

"And where d'you think you're going?" Maggie asked.

"I'm going to see if Mrs. O'Gorman will let me take Timmie for a walk."

"Are ye daft now? They'll soon be giving us something to eat at the lodging house. Come back with me at once." She reached toward Annie, but her sister skipped away from her grasp. "I'm not hungry. I'll just see Timmie for a while."

For all her squareness of build, Annie could run like a streak when she wanted to. Furthermore, she knew all kinds of back alleys leading to the street where Mrs. O'Gorman and Timmie lived.

It took Maggie another twenty minutes to find Annie sitting on the step of the side door of the Green Harp stroking Timmie and making him reach for a bone. When Maggie tried to pull Annie away there was a fearful commotion. Annie screamed, Timmie barked, and Mrs. O'Gorman came out.

"And what d'ye think yer doin?" she asked Maggie. "And please be kind enough to leave me dog alone. He's doin ye no harm." She yanked Maggie's hand away from its hold on Timmie's collar. "Annie, luv, now give over!"

"She's making me go away!" Annie howled. "She's letting those people take us on a boat and a train away from Ma and you and Timmie and New York."

"Aye. So I've heard." Mrs. O'Gorman frowned at Maggie. "Yer know, I've a mind to keep Annie meself. She'd be good with Timmie when I'm not home to take care of him."

"And what happens when she gets older?" Maggie said. "Will she go on the streets like . . . like . . . other girls who have no parents?" There was gossip to the effect that that was the way Mrs. O'Gorman herself had once earned her living. But Maggie didn't quite have the courage to say so.

Mrs. O'Gorman's face went red. Her lips narrowed. She was a heavy woman, though shapely. But next to the image of her mother that suddenly sprang to Maggie's mind, Mrs. O'Gorman looked coarse.

"And I suppose ye think that to take the child away out west will make everything right for the both of ye, Miss Prim and Proper! Does Father O'Mara know what ye'll be doing? It was Annie that was lighting the candles and making the novenas. Perhaps I'll be telling him."

"Ma said she wanted us to go out there. Didn't she say so, Annie? Ye heard her!"

Annie started to sing a little jig, tapping her feet. She lifted Timmie by his front paws and pretended she was dancing with him.

"Ye want to go out west with them Protestants?" Mrs. O'Gorman said. "Then go! But Annie doesn't have to go."

Maggie realized at that point that she had no power to make Annie go with her, not with Mrs. O'Gorman sitting there.

She swung around and faced the woman. "And you'll be taking care of Annie, and paying for her and sending her to school and getting the doctor to her when she's sick? Ye'll be doing all this the same as if she was yours?"

Mrs. O'Gorman hesitated, aware suddenly that she hadn't thought the matter through. Seeing her hesitation, Maggie acted. Turning on her heel, she walked away. Then she stopped and picked up a stick lying at the side of the dirty street.

"Here, Timmie!" she called, as she'd seen Annie do a dozen times. "Here!" And she threw the stick away from where Annie and Mrs. O'Gorman were sitting.

Timmie, who was still young enough to be intensely curious about everything, ran past her, followed immediately by Annie.

Maggie caught Annie as she ran by. Then, when Timmie, the stick in his mouth, came back towards her, she threw the stick back to where Mrs. O'Gorman was sitting. Timmie took off. But Maggie held onto Annie.

Whether it would work or not she didn't know, but she said in a low voice, "Ye have to go out west with me. Ye know it's what Ma wants. She said so. And if . . . if . . . Ma dies, there's nobody but me to take care of ye. If you stay with Mrs. O'Gorman, ye'll be going against Ma. And she said she'd be with the Blessed Virgin watching over us to see that we were doing what she told us to do."

It wasn't exactly what Mrs. Lavin had said, and Maggie's conscience gave a painful throb. But it was for Annie's own good, she silently argued. It was what Ma wanted. She repeated it to herself as though it were a litany.

"What d'ye mean, if Ma dies?" Annie turned her face towards Maggie. "What're ye sayin', Mag?"

"Annie, Ma's sick. Ye know that. Ye saw her taken away by the men from the hospital. She said . . . she said she didn't think she'd live. . . ." This violated Maggie's determination not to let herself think of anything except her mother's getting well. It was almost like letting her mother die, saying this to Annie. But Annie had to come back with her. She mustn't stay with Mrs. O'Gorman. "Annie, Ma'll be with the Blessed Virgin. She'll be watching over us when we go out west."

Annie continued to stare. Then she gave a wail. "Ma's gonna be dead!" she cried. "Dead." Her voice rose towards a scream.

"Annie, I'll take care of you. I promise. Just like Ma said. We'll be fine. And Ma'll be watching over us. Come back to the lodging house now, where they'll give us a bite to eat soon."

Praying that Mrs. O'Gorman wouldn't follow, Maggie led the sobbing Annie back towards the lodging house.

As though heaven had heard Mrs. Lavin's pleas and prayers and decided to take a hand to help her, a girl Maggie had grown up with, only a year older than herself, turned the corner and started coming down the opposite side of the street. Around her neck and despite the weather she wore a ragged piece of fur. She had on a long, cheap-looking, imitation silk skirt and leather boots, and she carried a reticule.

"Hello, Maggie," she said.

"Hello, Mary. How are you?"

"I'm fine, thank you. Just grand. Did ye see me fur?" and with one rather dirty hand she stroked it.

"And what did you have to do to get it?" Maggie asked.

Mary tossed her head. "Nothing that you won't be doing before long, Maggie me girl. Unless, of course, ye're going to be going for a nun."

"I'm not going to be going for a nun, Mary, and I'm not going to be selling meself on the streets, either. Annie and I, we're going west."

A wistful look came over Mary's face for a moment. Then she straightened. "Ah, it'll be the same out there. Ye'll see. I've a fine friend now who takes care of everything."

"Does he have a little dog?" Annie asked, her tears forgotten.

"He has a grand big one that fights in dog-fights and wins money for him."

"Come along, Annie," Maggie said. "We have to hurry."

27

Annie turned her face back towards the Green Harp as Maggie tugged. But Mrs. O'Gorman and Timmie had gone from the doorstep.

"Me friend would be glad to find ye a friend, Maggie. Ye're not bad-looking at all. And then we could be friends again."

"Annie and I'll not be friends with the likes of you now," Maggie said. She paused, sorry for the words and the tone. It seemed now a long time ago, but she had really liked Mary. "It's not that we weren't friends. And I'll think of you. But Annie and I have to go on the train."

Mary shrugged. "Do what you wish. But I hear the men out there are rough and cruel, and they don't have any money."

"Good-bye," Maggie said firmly. "Come along, Annie. We'll be getting back now." And they walked back. Annie seemed in a daze and stumbled now and again with the quick pace that Maggie was setting. But it was almost as though Maggie had started on the journey herself, and had to run to be sure they'd be ready for the train.

Three

Maggie stared out the window of the train and watched the trees and fields slide by. Annie, sitting beside Maggie, was humming one of her little tunes. It meant, Maggie reflected, with a stab of irritation, that Annie was probably thinking about Timmie and Mrs. O'Gorman. Sister Catherine had said Annie had a head full of pictures, and Mrs. Lavin had agreed, which meant, in practical terms, that any time Annie did not like her surroundings or was bored with what she was doing — or supposed to be doing — she would drift into fantasies of something she did like. This also resulted in her being useless in helping Maggie in the kitchen or taking care of Ma.

Then Annie stopped humming and asked, for the second time in an hour, "How long do you think it's going to be now, Maggie?"

"I told you, Annie, it's going to be days, maybe weeks. We have to go to many towns so the people there can see the children and decide who they want to adopt. Miss Trent told us how it would be."

Miss Trent, who was sitting at the back of the carriage where she could keep an eye on the twenty-seven children she was escorting, had explained the procedure to all of them.

The train, she said, would head west through New York State, down through Ohio and Kansas and would stop in towns along the way. An agent for the Children's Aid Society had gone ahead and had established the fact that individuals and families in those towns wanted to adopt children. When the train reached the towns she and the children would either line up on the station platform where the people of the town could see them and make a choice, or they would go into the town and use a church hall for the same purpose.

Like cattle at a fair. The words had popped into Maggie's mind before she knew she was thinking them. They came from memories of the days before she and her mother and father had left Ireland and Annie was still a baby.

"And," Miss Trent had reassured the assembled children, "these people have said they definitely wanted to adopt you, or we wouldn't be taking you, so I want you to look as cheerful as you can."

Maggie looked now at the faces of the other children sitting on the wooden seats in the train. There were sixteen boys and eleven girls, including herself and Annie. The oldest boy was fourteen, a tall, red-haired lad who didn't say much. Then there were several more boys who were eleven, twelve and thirteen. Somehow, without anyone from the Society having said so, the children were sure that these boys would have no trouble getting adopted. "They'll be for work on the farm," one of the girls had said.

Miss Trent had overheard the remark and said immediately, "No child placed by the Children's Aid Society is being adopted purely for work. We've been as careful as we know how to make sure of that. All those who want to adopt you have been vouched for by the local minister or other reliable people. Of course you will be expected to help out with chores, particularly those of you who will live on farms. But I want to assure you that agents from the Society will come by all the homes later to make certain that no child is being exploited. Your future parents sign agreements that they will ask of you no more than they would of their own children, and if we find that they are breaking that agreement, we'll take you away immediately and find you other homes."

Maggie wanted to believe her. She agreed with Tony, the dark, skinny, ragged boy who had never known any parents, and who shrugged and said, "It's better than sleeping in doorways."

But not all the children felt that way.

"Me ma said ye c'd nivver believe what those grand people said," one sharp-faced girl had said. "All that sweet talk about the poor, then they arrest some starvin' Irish maid who takes home food from their kitchen to feed her children."

Mrs. Lavin, who had been rebuked by the lady of the house where she was working for doing just that, had said the same.

"Maggie, they throw away stuff — eggs and bread and meat from their plates — that they don't eat. But if you slip a little of it into a bag to take home, then you're called a thief and Irish trash and dismissed!"

Staring out the train window at the darkening field, Maggie was thinking about that when Annie said suddenly, "When will Ma come and get us?"

Maggie felt her eyes filling.

* * *

32

A few days after they had come to the lodging, Miss Trent had come to Maggie and taken her into the little office off the main hall. Then holding her hand and speaking gently she had told Maggie that Mrs. Lavin had died.

"I'm so sorry, Maggie. But she was very ill, and now she's not suffering anymore."

Before Maggie actually heard the words, she knew Ma had died.

"No!" she cried. It was a terrible blow. Even though she'd known how ill Ma was, something within her had kept hoping that the doctors and the medicine would make her better, and she could come out west and be with them. Now Maggie knew she would never see her mother again.

"No," she said again, and then, "Ma . . ." She put her hands up to her face.

"I am so sorry," Miss Trent said gently. And then, after a minute, "Even before she . . . even before, she wanted you and Annie to get out of the city and away from the streets. I'm sure she is now very happy to know that you and Annie will be . . . will find a home out west. We were going to keep you here until the next train, seeing as your ma was still alive. But now, you can go on the one that leaves day after tomorrow."

"Yes," Maggie had repeated numbly, putting

33

her hands down. "It was what Ma wanted."

As she spoke her mother's name, she drew in her breath sharply and felt the tears in her eyes. She opened them as wide as she could, so they wouldn't spill over. Miss Trent's voice and angular face were kind, but it became important to Maggie that she not cry in front of this rich lady. Because for all her plain clothes, Miss Trent exuded a quality that to Maggie and the other children meant wealth. She spoke in quiet tones, never yelled or screamed, and used genteel words even when she was annoyed. One day, Maggie was determined, she would be that way herself. But for now, it put a barrier between the likes of Miss Trent and the children she was taking west.

"Would you like me to tell Annie, or would you prefer to tell her yourself?" Miss Trent asked.

"I'll tell her," Maggie said. "I'll tell her when it's right." Then she blurted out something that had been worrying her a great deal. "Are you sure there'll be a family that will take both of us? We have to stay together. Annie . . . Annie couldn't stay with strange people alone."

Miss Trent hesitated. "I can't be absolutely certain about that, Maggie, but I can promise you that we won't let you and Annie be adopted until we find a family that wants to take you both. That was the promise we made Mrs. Lavin, and we wouldn't break it."

"Did you see Ma?"

"No. But Dr. Purdy was with her when she died, and I know she asked that, and he promised for us."

Maggie paused. Miss Trent, of course, was a Protestant and couldn't be expected to understand Maggie's next question. Still, she had to ask it. "Will there be a Mass for her?"

"I believe so. Someone was sending for the priest when Dr. Purdy left."

They were both silent. Maggie pushed open her eyes as wide as they'd go, forcing the tears welling up again not to fall. She was sure that if she asked if she and Annie could attend the Mass for Ma, they would be allowed to. But she was also certain that if they did, Father O'Mara would find out about their going west on the train and would do his best to stop them. And then they would not be able to do as Ma had wanted.

"Would you like to stay here in the office a while by yourself?" Miss Trent asked. "You can come out just before supper."

"Thank you," Maggie whispered.

After Miss Trent had left, Maggie let herself cry. "Ma," she whispered. "Ma."

She tried to imagine her with the Blessed

Virgin, but it wasn't easy. In every statue and picture Maggie had ever seen, the Blessed Virgin had looked young and untroubled, frequently smiling, her blue cloak no bluer than her eyes. Mrs. Lavin's eyes were blue, too. But her face was gaunt and lined and some of her teeth were gone. And in the last few terrible months her skin had been gray, and her mouth more often than not flecked with blood. To summon up a picture of her wasted mother and the doll-like Virgin sitting together was more than Maggie could manage.

"It's not right," Maggie sobbed to herself. She knew that Father O'Mara would say that in heaven her mother would be with the Virgin and be well again and would look as she had as a girl. But she also knew she didn't believe him, and a great anger against him and the Church and the Blessed Virgin filled her. Then she saw she had committed a mortal sin and there, standing alone in the little office of the Protestant lodging house, she quickly said a Hail Mary.

The loss and the anger were still with her as, holding Annie firmly by the hand, she had gone with Miss Trent and the other children on the boat to Albany and then taken the train going west. During that time the moment to tell Annie about their mother's death had never been right. Maggie told herself it was because she didn't want Annie to grieve until they had been on their journey for a while, but she also knew that she wanted to refrain from telling Annie until the sights and smells and sounds of New York were far behind them.

The journey up the Hudson past the docks and the boats had been exciting. The boys had raced up and down the deck and had tried to go into the wheelhouse with the pilot. Annie had wanted to run with them, and because Maggie was eager to put off the moment when she had to tell Annie about Ma's death, Maggie had let her run, following to keep an eye on her and stop her from falling off the boat.

They had spent the night on the boat, huddled onto the seats, and then had eaten the breakfast that Miss Trent had arranged for them to have the next morning. When they had finished, they left the boat and were led across the city of Albany to the train station. A car in the train had been reserved for them, and they sat there, chattering excitedly, until, after a great burst of steam and some shouting and whistle blowing, the train pulled out.

"And now, children," Miss Trent said, walking up and down the aisle, "it's going to be a long trip, longer perhaps than any of you have taken, so I want you to be as patient as you can. Watch the scenery from the window. It will be all new country to you."

They all tried. Maggie kept pointing out things to Annie as they passed them — farmhouses, barns, horses, cows, people, wagons, creeks, children running along with the train, and Annie responded by keeping up a running prattle about each one.

But after several hours and a long period of tired silence, she suddenly complained, "This seat's hard."

"Be grateful," Miss Trent, who was on one of her walks up and down the car, had replied before Maggie could say anything. "They used to make us travel in a freight cart. We all had to sit on the floor."

By the afternoon they were far beyond the city or any town. Maggie, watching the grass and trees and farmhouses and meadows go by, was reminded of Ireland, though the green in Ireland was greener, and there weren't as many trees in the county they had come from, and the little houses were poorer. Would Ma have lived if they could have got beyond the streets of New York and made their home here in the open country? She was pondering this when Annie suddenly asked her question: "When will Ma come and get us?"

Maggie thought for a moment of putting her off. But they were going to be on this train a long time. There was no private room they could go to. And Maggie was tired. The pain inside her was heavy around her heart.

"Ma's dead, Annie," she said and took her sister's hand. "She's with the Blessed Virgin."

Annie stared at her for a moment. Then her mouth opened in a loud wail. She snatched her hand away. "No, Mag. She's not. She's not dead." Annie's grubby fingers tugged at Maggie's sleeve. "She's not dead, now, is she?"

"Yes, Annie. I told you. She's with the Blessed Virgin, and they're watching us as we go on the train to find a new home, just the way Ma wanted. You know she wanted that!"

Annie began to weep and howl. The other children crowded around. "My mother died," Lawrence said.

"I never had no mother," Tony said.

"That's stupid. You had to have a mother," the sharp-voiced girl said. "Everybody has one."

"Well I didn't!"

"You just — "

But at that point, seeing that Annie was still sobbing, Miss Trent made the children all go back to their seats.

"Now, Annie," she said in a kind voice. "Your

mother is well now, and you and Maggie are doing what she wanted you to do, aren't you?"

But Annie ignored her. She sobbed and hiccoughed, her eyes and nose running. "You shoulda told me, Mag! You shoulda told me! I could have gone to her. She wouldn't have died! It's your fault!"

The words hurt. Part of Maggie wanted to cry again with Annie and, like her sister, blame somebody. Instead she put her arm around her and said, "There now, Annie. We're doing what Ma wanted us to do."

"Of course it's not your sister's fault, Annie," Miss Trent said, a little shocked. "Your mother wanted you two to be together and to come on the train with us!"

After what seemed to Maggie a long time, Annie, worn out, finally stopped. Miss Trent, aware of having ignored the others for too long, slipped away. Maggie, exhausted and fearful, sat silent beside her sister. Finally she said, "It'll be all right, Annie. I promise you. You'll see. We'll be out in the green with the grass and the trees and nice people."

It was the wrong thing to say. "I want to go back to New York," Annie said.

"We can't go back," Maggie said trying to sound reasonable. "There's no place for us to go." And then she could have bitten her tongue, because she had given Annie the lead her sister now took.

"We can go live with Mrs. O'Gorman and Timmie. I'm sure she'd find a place for you, and you could work in the Green Harp, and I can take care of Timmie."

"No," Maggie said. "Ma wouldn't want that." And then, as Annie's eyes filled again and her mouth opened, Maggie said harshly, "It's true, you know it's true. Ma wouldn't want us in New York, and she wouldn't want us with Mrs. O'Gorman, so it's no use your talking about it."

Annie started to cry again, but quietly this time. Maggie, sorry for the way she had spoken, put her arms around Annie. "There now," she said. "There now."

After that, Annie slept.

For the next several days, as the train rolled west, Annie slept and stared out the window and periodically cried as she remembered or talked about Ma or Mrs. O'Gorman or Timmie or New York. Then one day, when the train had stopped, and they were out on the station platform stretching their legs, Annie saw a small dog in the charge of somebody who had come to meet the train. Before Maggie could think to stop her, she'd run up to the dog and started petting it.

The man holding the dog on its leash was amused and indulgent as Annie stroked the short tan coat of the dog. When she asked if she could take the dog with her on the train for awhile, he smiled and shook his head. "The train might go off, and then I'd be without my dog. You must ask your parents to give you one of your own. Where are they?" And he looked around.

At that moment the guard blew the whistle and Maggie, who had lost Annie, came rushing up and pulled her away. "We have to get back on the train. It's about to go."

"But I want to play with the little dog."

"No!" Maggie dragged the reluctant Annie back towards the train and was then joined and helped by a worried Miss Trent.

"Get her a dog of her own!" the dog owner called as they climbed into the car.

"We almost missed the train," Maggie said.

"Can I have a dog of my own, Mag, when we get out west?"

"We'll have to ask the people we live with, Annie. If they say yes, you can."

For the first time since she had learned of her mother's death, Annie smiled. "That'd be grand!"

Four

The days became weeks. They had been traveling on the train now for more than a month. Maggie had become used to the routine.

They would come to a town where the Society had learned there were people — farmers, business people, lawyers, doctors and ministers — who were interested in adopting one or more of the children, and had been vouched for by an agent of the Society or a local minister or by reliable fellow citizens.

When the train pulled in Miss Trent ushered the children out onto the platform, counted them and then found out from whoever was meeting them — a local agent or possibly a citizen with whom she had corresponded — where the children and the townspeople were supposed to meet.

43

Wherever the meetings took place, on the platforms or in church halls, Maggie came to think of those hours as cattle fairs. She could feel her spine stiffen with pride as she stood, holding Annie by the hand, while the people came to peer and point. Then she would remember Father O'Mara thundering from the pulpit at Mass that pride was the deadliest of all the sins and remind herself that their being there was what Ma wanted.

When the children were lined up Miss Trent introduced them by name, and then read the agreement that all adoptive parents would be expected to sign and to adhere to.

After that she delivered a short speech that Maggie came to know by heart.

"The Reverend Mr. Brace believes — and all of us who have worked with him know he is right — that no matter what the child's previous condition, a kind home, with affection, reasonable discipline and good schooling can make responsible citizens of all of these young ones. All they need is a chance." And always, after she had said that, Miss Trent's kind, plain face lit up with the strength of her hope and her conviction.

Mostly the children stood silent. Maggie tried to remember that Miss Trent had told them to look cheerful. Annie sometimes stared ahead at the people. More often she looked down at her feet. Maggie came to pray she would catch sight of a small dog somewhere, because when she did her face would light up. Even though afterwards it was hard to get Annie back on the train without the dog, Maggie believed it improved the chances of their adoption.

Miss Trent had told Maggie that there was a couple in Kansas that had expressed interest in her, but had said nothing about Annie. So, determined they should be taken together, Maggie blessed any chance that put a smile on Annie's face. Whenever the gaze of anyone of the people who had met the train came to rest on her own face, Maggie smiled. If she and Annie could smile together, Maggie believed, then someone might want the two of them. Occasionally she prayed to the Blessed Virgin that this would be so. But then, when she tried to imagine her mother with Da and the Blessed Virgin, she ran into the same difficulties she had before. They didn't fit into the same mental picture.

At night, when the train windows were black with the dark, and there were no houses and no lights, and Annie was asleep, Maggie would sometimes worry that her problems with her mother and the Blessed Virgin had come about because she had sinned. And she would then say extra Hail Marys for forgiveness, for the hope that she and Annie would find a home, for Ma, who was there with God and the Blessed Virgin, even if Maggie couldn't imagine them together.

Sometimes, when Miss Trent had finished her speech, Maggie would hear a half-stifled cynical whisper — most frequently from a dark thin boy with angry black eyes.

On one occasion, when Miss Trent had finished talking, Maggie, who was standing right in front of the boy, heard him mutter, "A fat chance we'll have with this lot! They look like they'd rather sell us for meat!"

"Shut up, Roberto!" the boy with the short leg whispered. "If you don't want to be adopted, I do. This is farming country, and I want to be a farmer."

"With that leg? Farmers need strong boys!"

Miss Trent turned. "All right, children. Now try not to talk, and turn around so that these good people can see you."

Maggie had to admit that Roberto had a point. She stared at the stolid faces, the women's round and pink under their bonnets, and the men's often almost invisible behind beards.

But then she suffered a shock, because the

most indifferent-looking man stepped up to Roberto and said in a gentle voice, "Would you like to come with us, son? We'll try to be good to you!"

And Roberto, the tough, had to swallow several times before he said in a meeker voice than anyone had heard him use, "Yes, sir. Thank you, sir."

Slowly, as the days passed, and they gathered again and again on station platforms or in town or church halls, other children were taken, and Maggie watched their faces light up and saw them go off with their new parents.

But no one took Lawrence, the boy with the short leg. One man came up, but when he saw Lawrence whole, he noticed the obviously shorter leg. He didn't say anything. Just shook his head. Lawrence said, as soon as they were back on the train, "I didn't like him anyway."

It wasn't until they were down to seven that the possibility Maggie had dreaded became a reality. A pleasant young couple wanted to adopt Annie — and only Annie.

"I'm sorry. That's impossible," Miss Trent said quickly. "Maggie and Annie are sisters, and they have to be taken together."

"We can't afford to take them both," the

young man said. "But we'd love to have Goldilocks here. She's . . . she's sort of like the daughter we lost."

The matter could have been solved more easily if at that moment a small white-and-tan terrier hadn't run up.

"Look — a little dog," Annie said, and ran after the puppy as it circled around the people.

"This is Ginger," the young wife said. And then, "Did you have a dog of your own?"

Annie bent down to pat the dog. "He was Mrs. O'Gorman's, but she let me look after him, and he liked me a lot. His name was Timmie. He always came when I called him." Her voice, which had been bright and steady, wavered.

"If you come live with us, we'll give you Ginger to play with."

"Oh, please don't say that," Miss Trent said belatedly. But it was no use.

"I'll come to live with you. Can I have Ginger right now?"

"I'm sorry," Maggie said. "You can't have Annie. I promised Ma that we'd be adopted together. And there's a family in Kansas that wants us, isn't there, Miss Trent?" Maggie remembered perfectly well what Miss Trent had said, but she was frightened and hoped that

Miss Trent would support her in this.

But Miss Trent was a realist. "They didn't say anything about Annie."

"I won't let Annie go," Maggie said. Her voice was steady, but within her the fear was growing that somehow Annie could be taken from her, that they would be separated without her being able to stop it.

"No, I wouldn't ask you to do that. If worse comes to worst we can perhaps board you with some people until we find someone willing to give you a permanent home." Miss Trent looked at the young couple rather wistfully. "I certainly don't want to urge you to do something that you feel you cannot afford. But are you sure you could only take the one?"

The wife looked pleadingly at her husband. But he shook his head. "You know I'd do it for you if I could, Dora. But we just can't. I'd be happy to take Annie here, but that's all I can do."

Ginger had come back and was dancing on his hind legs trying to reach the stick Annie was holding above his head. "You wouldn't mind if I call him Timmie?" Annie asked. Maggie, who knew well Annie's ability not to hear what she didn't want to hear, felt like slapping her.

"No, honey," the wife said. "You can call him

anything you like. He's so young he probably isn't used to any name yet."

"I am sorry," Miss Trent said. "I cannot allow the sisters to be separated."

"She said I could call him Timmie," Annie said to Maggie.

"You never listen to anything except what you want to hear," Maggie said, almost in tears. "Didn't ye mind what she was saying? That they couldn't take us both?"

"But you'd come back, wouldn't you?" Annie lifted her face to Maggie. "You're not going to die like Ma, Mag, are you?" Suddenly her face crumpled. Maggie stared into the enormous slate-blue eyes so much like their mother's. Annie's voice rose. "You're not going to die, Mag! Say you're not!"

For a moment Maggie felt a fierce satisfaction. So, when she could be forced to pay attention, Annie did not want to be separated from her! Then she felt ashamed, and put her arms around her sister. "Of course I'm not going to die. But we've got to go farther on now, where there'll be a home for both of us."

"Timmie?" Annie asked.

"Timmie's back in New York," Maggie said as patiently as she could. "Maybe when we get to Kansas there'll be a Timmie there for you."

"Promise?"

"No, Annie, I can't promise. You know I can't."

"We're going to have to go back to the train now," Miss Trent spoke, not without a note of relief. "People have chosen their children and have signed the papers and are ready to leave. And I have food for our supper. Annie, please try to stop crying! You know you'd hate to be without your sister."

But Annie whimpered until they were in the train and were sitting down, at which point she sat silent with large tears rolling down her cheeks.

"Come along now, Annie," Maggie said, exasperated. "Who do you love — Timmie or me?"

"You know I love you, Maggie. But Timmie loves me."

"And don't you think I love you — you silly child!"

"But I make you cross. I never made Timmie cross."

It was said innocently, with no suggestion of reproach. But Maggie felt rebuked nevertheless. Something must have shown on her face, because Annie said anxiously, "Maggie?"

"Yes, Annie."

"Ye're not cross with me again?"

"No. But sometimes you'd try the patience of a saint."

"That's what Ma always said."

More children were adopted. Outside, the land became flat and brown.

"Why is it so brown?" Lawrence asked.

"Because the harvest is already over," Miss Trent said. She had changed her seat to be near the remaining children. "And if there is a winter crop, it's probably too soon to have been planted. Or if it has been planted, it's too soon to show."

The neat furrows, one after the other in parallel lines, went to the horizon. Here and there a few trees would rise up in the middle of the flatness.

"It doesn't look like New York," Annie said. "Aren't there any people here?"

"The people here don't live as close together as we did in New York. It's much better this way, you know, Annie. People here have a chance to breathe properly."

"I breathed fine in New York."

"That's not true, Annie," Maggie said. "You had a lot of colds. Don't you remember?"

Annie didn't say anything.

"Come on, Annie," Maggie said. "Now breathe in like this." And Maggie sucked in a great breath of air, holding it. Then she let it out. "See if you can do that."

Obediently Annie breathed in deeply and then exhaled.

"Now don't you remember, Annie, the time when Sister Scolastica made you stand in the corner at Sunday school because you breathed with your mouth open?"

"Sister Scolastica didn't like dogs. She said they didn't have souls and wouldn't go to heaven," Annie said.

"You should tell her about St. Francis," Miss Trent said. "Now there's a saint who loved all creatures — dogs, birds, wolves. There's a legend somewhere about how he made friends with a wolf that was ravaging the town of Gubbio in Italy. But when they sent for St. Francis, he made friends with the wolf and then told it that it mustn't molest the townsfolk."

"Did the wolf stop doing it?" Maggie asked skeptically.

"According to the stories — yes." She glanced at Maggie curiously. "You were raised a Catholic. Haven't you heard of him?"

"There's a church of St. Francis in New York, but it's not near us. We were told that he was a great saint for the Faith, but not that part about the wolf."

"I'll tell Annie," Miss Trent said. "She'd like some of the stories."

After a period of silence, Maggie, who was staring out the window, said, "I like the way it's flat here, so you can see for miles."

"You sometimes talk as though you remember something beside New York. Where did your family come from?"

"Kildare. I was born there. But we left when I was six."

"And you remember it?"

"I just remember the green fields, and air that blew all the time and was fresh. Ma used to talk about it. But it made her sad and angry, because our cottage was burned and all our animals killed."

"Because your father was involved in a rebellion?"

"No, because the lord of the land — we never saw him, mind. He was almost never there — but he wanted the land for his fine horses. Me da refused to go. That's why the estate manager burned our cottage. Then we had to go. We had nothing."

Towns drifted past. The countryside became even flatter. And one by one all the children except Lawrence, Maggie and Annie were adopted. Then, in a town in Missouri, when

Miss Trent ushered the three children out onto the platform, there was a large man with his wife standing there. They wanted to adopt Lawrence.

"One of my legs is shorter than the other," Lawrence said, before Miss Trent could say anything. His face was white.

The wife laughed, showing dimples in her plump cheeks. "We don't think that's a problem."

The man smiled. He was a little older than the other men who had adopted children. "Walk towards me, son."

Lawrence walked towards him, dipping at every other step.

"Let me show you something," the man said when Lawrence stopped. And he turned and walked past them, his limp as pronounced as Lawrence's. "I have a bad leg, too," he said. "So don't worry. I'm a lawyer, but I have a few animals and my wife here could use a little help. My leg doesn't bother me at all, and I don't think yours will. So how about it?"

Lawrence gave a shakey smile, his mouth quivering a little. "I'd like that," he said.

The man's stout, kind wife smiled back. "We'd like it, too."

Lawrence turned to Maggie. "I sure hope you both get taken," he said.

"Yes." Maggie squeezed his hand. "They look nice," she whispered.

" 'Bye, Annie," he said.

" 'Bye."

In the remaining days Maggie kept telling herself that she and Annie would be fine, that the family in Kansas that wanted her would also take Annie. On gray days, when the gray sky seemed endless before them, her determined optimism faltered. Then she took hold of herself. She and Annie were doing what their mother wanted them to do. It would be all right.

Annie no longer said very much. She stared out the window and only spoke when Maggie or Miss Trent said something to her. She ate the food that Miss Trent arranged to have brought to the train. Maggie thought about Sister Catherine's remark: Annie has a head full of pictures.

"She seems very quiet," Miss Trent said to Maggie.

"Yes." Maggie was unhappy about it, but didn't know what to do or say.

"Never mind," Miss Trent said cheerfully. "She'll be better when . . . when you're with a family. She'll have something then to distract her, to stimulate her."

Maggie knew Miss Trent's hesitation came from her own doubt about their being adopted. As she had explained to Maggie, one way or another they'd be with a family. If they weren't adopted, they would be boarded out. But Maggie's heart sank when she allowed herself to think about the latter.

Then they pulled into the town of Melrose in Kansas, and went out to stand on the station platform. There, waiting for them, was a rather stern-looking man with his wife.

"These are the Russells," Miss Trent said as the two groups eyed one another. "They're the family I told you about."

Five

Maggie, looking at them, felt something within her quiver. Mr. Russell was tall and rather lean. He had on a black hat and a wool coat and boots. His beard, which was short and trimmed, prevented her from seeing the lower half of his face, and the brim of his hat seemed to put the rest of it in shadow, but she thought he had dark eyes. Maggie gripped Annie's hand.

"Is this the little girl?" the man asked in a deep voice.

"These are Maggie and Annie Lavin," Miss Trent said. "Maggie is twelve and Annie is seven." She stopped.

"Come here, Maggie," the man said.

Maggie hesitated for an instant. If she let go of Annie's hand, they might think she was willing to be adopted by herself. But if she didn't do as he asked, he might not want either of them. Releasing Annie's hand, she walked forward.

Mr. Russell stared down at her for a moment. Then he indicated the woman standing next to him. "This is my wife."

Maggie looked at the woman. She, also, was fairly tall, but she was thin, and there was a frailty about her that seemed to show in the hollows in her cheeks, and in her slender hands.

"How do you do?" Maggie said.

Mrs. Russell smiled then. Her eyes were gray and the hair that showed under the sunbonnet was a light brown. "How do you do, Maggie? Would you — would you like to come and live with us?"

Maggie felt her heart leap towards the woman, but she said in a firm voice, "I cannot leave my sister, Annie. Ma left her in my charge."

"We wrote we only wanted one girl," Mr. Russell said. "My wife has been ill, and we have my mother-in-law living with us. She is now mostly bedridden. My wife needs help with the chores. But a seven-year-old is not old enough to be of help."

There was a silence. Miss Trent, standing with Annie, watched them.

Then the man said, "Don't you want to come

and make your home with us? We will be good to you, I promise."

In her mind Maggie heard her mother's voice saying, "Maybe it's God's way of sending you west, out of the filth and the slum."

The air on the station platform was blown by a sharp, fresh wind. Beyond the station, Maggie could see trees and a street with a few houses on either side. She knew this was the end of the line for herself and Annie. After this they would return. They would be boarded with people who would have to be paid to keep them. She swallowed and pushed back a small, furtive satisfaction that, unlike many people who were charmed with Annie, here was a couple who wanted Maggie for herself. She told herself it was easy to see why they — or at least Mr. Russell — did: He needed a worker who could help his rather frail-looking wife. But everything deepest and most elemental in Maggie condemned that feeling as selfish. Ma had left her in charge of Annie.

"No. I can't stay here without Annie. She's got no one but me to care for her." And she turned and walked back to where Miss Trent and Annie were standing.

The man's stern mouth seemed to be a straight line. He said to Miss Trent, "I think you should have told us that the girl could not be adopted without another child."

Miss Trent hesitated. "Yes, I probably should have. I did say in my letter that there were two of them, and I suppose I hoped that you'd change your mind."

"Don't you like me?" Annie said.

Mr. Russell turned toward her, a little surprised. "It's not a question of liking — er — what is your name?"

"Annie," his wife said.

"It's not a question of liking you, Annie. It's just the amount of room we have and the work that needs to be done."

"We have room," Mrs. Russell said. "The two girls can sleep together in the main room. We planned to put one girl there. There's plenty of room for two. They can have their bed in the corner."

"I think we ought to discuss this," Mr. Russell said firmly, "in private."

His wife turned to him. "James, if we don't take them now, they'll have to go back on the train, isn't that so?"

"Yes," Miss Trent said. "We turn around here. It would be wonderful — " She stopped. "I shouldn't try to overpersuade you."

"Do you have a dog?" Annie asked.

For the first time the man smiled. "Yes. We have a dog. He guards our place. Do you like dogs?"

"I used to take care of Timmie. He belonged

61

to Mrs. O'Gorman. When she had to work she'd leave him with me."

"James," Mrs. Russell said. There was a plea in her voice.

He turned and looked at her. "I'm just afraid that such a small child will be a burden. And you mustn't have more than you can manage. I don't want you ill again, Priscilla."

"I won't be ill again. I do need help, especially with Mother." She hesitated. "Annie will grow, you know. And if we don't take both girls, we'll have none."

He stood for a minute, looking at his wife, then at Maggie and Annie. "All right," he said. "All right."

Saying good-bye to Miss Trent was surprisingly hard. Much as she hated their life in New York, Maggie suddenly realized that Miss Trent was the last link with all that she'd known since she was six, and with Ma.

"You'll be back to see us?" she asked.

"If the Society sends me back. They send people to see all our children. But I don't know whether it'll be me." She bent and hugged Annie. "Now, Annie, be a good girl. Do what Maggie and the Russells say. Promise?"

Annie grinned. "Yes."

"Maggie . . ." Miss Trent gave Maggie a quick

hug. "Write to me if you get a chance. I'm sure that everything is going to be just the way your mother wanted for you. But I'd love to hear in detail." She saw Maggie's hesitation.

Maggie said, "I'm not that good with the letters, but I'll learn, and then I'll write."

"Of course."

"Haven't the children been to school?" Mr. Russell said.

Miss Trent glanced towards Maggie, who said quickly, "We had to take care of Ma. Annie here, she hasn't been to school except with the nuns. I was, a little. But there wasn't a school when I was younger."

"I see. Well, Mrs. Russell, here, was once a schoolteacher. I'm sure she'd help you — when she has time." He glanced at Miss Trent. "Are you going back on the train right away?"

"Yes. It will take me to Independence, then I'll get another train back to New York. You have some papers to sign, so I suppose we'd better do that."

Mr. and Mrs. Russell sat up on the bench behind the horses. Mr. Russell drove, and Maggie and Annie sat on some straw in the wagon itself. It was early in the afternoon when they started out, and Maggie stared in curiosity at the little town, its frame houses, dirt road and all the horses tied up to hitching posts. People on the street and on the wooden sidewalk greeted the Russells, saying "Hiya, Jim," and "Evenin', Miz Russell." To Maggie's ears, it sounded very different from the accents of New York, more different, she thought suddenly, than even the Russells' way of talking.

Then the people's glances slid towards the wagon itself to where Maggie and Annie were sitting. Those tall enough looked over the sides of the wagon and examined the two strangers.

"These your new young'uns?" a man asked, then spat tobacco juice in an arc behind the wagon.

"Yes," Mrs. Russell said in a quiet, pleasant voice. "These are Maggie and Annie."

Mr. Russell didn't say anything.

Finally they left the town and started on a track across the prairie. Tall, waving grass stretched as far as they could see, and the wind, rippling over the grass, made it dip and sway, carrying sweet smells with it. Maggie, staring at the huge horizon, thought about the cramped room they — Ma, Annie and herself — had lived in. But thinking about Ma made Maggie more aware than ever that she was dead. They would never see her again. An aching sense of loss filled her.

"What're you thinking about?" Annie asked.

Shorter than Maggie, she couldn't see anything over the wagon side but sky.

"I was thinkin' of Ma," Maggie said. And then wondered if it would set Annie off.

"She's with the Blessed Virgin," Annie said.

Maggie saw Mr. Russell's face turn a little towards them, so they could see his profile for a moment. Then he turned forward again.

A while later, Annie, who had been half standing in the wagon, her elbows on the wagon side, suddenly said, "There's a doggie!"

Mrs. Russell turned quickly and looked. "No, Annie, honey, that's a jackrabbit."

"What's a rabbit?"

"Ye know very well, Annie, what a rabbit is," Maggie said. "I've told you meself, and Ma, when we were talking about Ireland."

"I think the rabbits in Ireland, like those in England, are smaller," Mr. Russell said.

"Have you been there — sir?" Maggie asked. "I mean, have you been to Ireland?"

"No. But I've read about the wild creatures there."

"Can I have one?" Annie said.

Mr. Russell laughed. "Maybe for dinner one night."

Everything looked so flat, Maggie thought, and yet, sometimes when she looked back at the track, she saw that they had dipped down. Once, when they had to cross a stream, they definitely descended, passing bluffs of yellow mud and thick clusters of trees. Near the water, flowers of red and yellow dotted the long grass.

Just as it was getting to be dusk, they saw a low, rather long house and another smaller one near it.

"That's home," Mr. Russell said.

"Home," Maggie repeated. Under her breath she said it again, trying to make it feel natural and real. But it didn't feel real. Not for her. For the Russells, yes, but not yet for her and Annie.

"Annie," she whispered, taking her sister's hand and pulling her down into the straw beside her. "We must be good now and help every way we can. Otherwise they might not want to keep us."

"Could we go back to New York, then?" Annie whispered back.

"No," Maggie said, hardening her heart. She knew that their only hope was for Annie not to be allowed even to think that they could go back. "No, we can never go back, Annie. This is our home. No matter what."

* * *

66

Maggie heard the barking before she saw the black-and-white guard dog. He started barking the moment they got off the main path and headed towards the house.

"That's Spot," Mr. Russell said. "He lets us know when anybody's coming around."

"*Spot!*" Annie said, staring over the side of the wagon.

The house was larger than Maggie had expected it to be from the distance. As they got closer she could see it was made of logs and seemed to be in two sections: a main part, and another, smaller part at one end. There was a wooden roof, windows of glass, and a front door with a latch. To the back and side was another house.

"Who lives in the other house?" she asked, as Mr. Russell helped her down out of the wagon.

"It's our barn. A cow, a calf and Rufus and Rumpkin, our horses, live there. We'll show you them tomorrow. Come along, Annie. Maybe I'd better just lift you out." And he did.

"Welcome home," Mrs. Russell said rather shyly, as they walked towards the front door. She pushed down the latch and they all went in.

It smelled different from any house Maggie had ever been in, and she wasn't sure what went into the smell, except for baking bread, which she recognized, and a strange odor that came from the smouldering fire in the fireplace.

The room was not large, but it was larger than the tenement room Maggie, Annie and their mother had lived in for so long. At one end was a door that obviously led to another room, and a table, some chairs and, fixed to the wall, a sink. At the other end, next to the fireplace, was another door that seemed to lead to the extension Maggie had seen from the outside.

"Now if you'll just hang up your coats on these pegs," Mrs. Russell said, "we'll get things going for supper."

Maggie was just hanging her shawl over the peg when she saw Annie disappear out the front door.

"Annie!" she called. "Annie, come back here!"

"Maybe she wants to go to the outhouse," Mrs. Russell said.

"She's after the dog, I'm sure," Maggie said, worried.

They both went outside the house and then around towards the back where the dog was.

Maggie saw Annie's figure, in its too-short coat, running towards what looked to Maggie like a large, fierce dog. When Annie was about ten feet away from him he lunged against the rope, his teeth bared. Annie stopped. At that moment, Mr. Russell came out of the barn.

"Watch out!" he called. "Come back from there. Spot's a guard dog and he can be savage."

Annie stared at the dog, a mostly white, stocky terrier with a big brindled patch on its side. A deep growl broke from his throat, and he lunged again.

Annie backed away slowly.

"Annie! Come here!" Maggie cried. "It's not like Timmie. It's fierce, to guard the house. Now come back!"

Annie finally turned and came back. She didn't say anything, but Maggie saw a bewildered, almost desolate look on her face.

Maggie was setting the table. Mrs. Russell had said, "We'll pull the table out from the wall there, and you can set it with the knives and forks that are in the second drawer in that bureau. We brought that bureau all the way from Washington," she said proudly.

"The capital?" Maggie asked.

"Yes, that's right."

Maggie wanted to ask why she was living here in a log cabin if she had been in Washington, but then she thought that perhaps Mrs. Russell, a little like Mrs. Lavin, had been too poor to have a place of her own.

"Were you very poor?" she said.

Mrs. Russell looked at her in some surprise, then smiled. "Not, not really, but James, my husband, had wanted to come out here to the frontier for a long time, and when he got out of the army that's when we came."

Maggie was over at the bureau, pulling open the drawer. Inside, wrapped in soft wool, were knives, forks and spoons. Maggie had never seen any cutlery at home except tin. But she had occasionally been with her mother in the big house in Washington Square, where Mrs. Lavin worked in the kitchen, when the silver had been brought back from the dining room to be washed, and her mother had pointed out the marks on the pieces that showed they were real silver. Surreptitiously she looked at the fork she was holding. Yes, there was the funny square mark.

Mrs. Russell had spread a white cloth on the table. "We don't always do this, Maggie, because we could get a tablecloth dirty every night without even trying hard, but tonight is special, because of you and Annie."

Again Maggie felt drawn to the slender woman now showing her how the silver was laid out. "We don't use the silver all the time, either," she said. "It's for special occasions like Thanksgiving and Christmas and — " she smiled shyly again — "and the time we gained our two daughters." She paused. "I do hope you'll be happy here. We — my husband and I — wanted children so much. But — it was not to be. So now we have you!"

The big pot on top of the fire was sending out a delicious smell when Mrs. Russell said, "I'm now going to prepare a tray for my mother. She isn't able to come to the table with us, so we'll take a tray in to her, and I'll introduce you." She paused. "I'll take Annie in later."

Quickly Mrs. Russell took a tray from behind the bureau and placed it near the hearth. She was about to lift the big ladle from the pot when she glanced at Maggie. "Here, now. You put some of the chicken stew from the big pot and some beans from the other pot onto the plate here, and then take a potato from the hot stones there. Use this cloth or you'll burn your fingers. Then put the plate on the tray while I pour Mother some coffee."

Maggie did as she was told and was about to turn back towards Mrs. Russell when she saw Annie's far from clean hand about to go into the stew. Hastily she snatched it away. "Now stop that, Annie," she said. "We must wait until we sit down."

Annie let out a wail.

"Now don't cry. We'll all be eating soon." Maggie was trying not to be impatient, but she wanted so much for Annie, whom the Russells hadn't really wanted, to make a good impression.

Mrs. Russell came over to Annie. "She's tired, Maggie. It's been a long journey. Come along now, Annie. I know you're hungry. Now just this once you can have a small bite while you're waiting." And Mrs. Russell took one of the small spoons from table, dipped it into the stew, and gave it to Annie. "See if this will fill your tummy until we sit down."

Annie took the spoon and put the whole bowl into her mouth. Then she opened her mouth and let it fall out. "Hot!" she said. "Hot!"

"Annie!" Maggie said, looking down onto the clean wooden floor, now spotted here and there with chicken stew.

"It was hot!" Annie said.

"Of course it was," Mrs. Russell said. "I should have told you to nibble it. Well, I'm afraid you're going to have to wait. Now take the — " Mrs. Russell seemed to change her mind. "Maggie, would you take the cloth from the bowl over there, damp it just a little, and wipe up the stew from the floor? I'll put a little wax on it tomorrow."

Maggie went over, dampened the cloth, and came and wiped up the stew. She was aware of being unreasonably upset with Annie, and while she wiped and wiped, tried to think of what Ma would have said.

"All right now. I've just poured the coffee. Let's take the tray into Mother." She picked up the tray, then, after a moment's thought, said to Maggie, "You can carry it."

She and Maggie started towards the door on the other side of the fireplace. At the door she turned, "Now, Annie, just sit on that bench there, and we'll be right out."

Maggie turned also, the tray in her hands. "Don't touch anything, Annie," she said.

The woman sitting up in bed had thin, finely shaped features, and gray hair gathered on top of her head and pinned in a braid. Underneath, her dark eyes were lively and piercing.

"Come in," she said. And then as Maggie walked over to the bed, "And who is this?"

"This is Maggie, who has come to live with us as our daughter," Mrs. Russell said.

Maggie was preoccupied with getting the tray straight and correctly placed.

"And Maggie," Mrs. Russell said, when the tray was safely down, "this is my mother, Mrs. Vanderpool."

"How do you do, ma'am," Maggie said, and

remembering lectures on manners by the nuns, dropped a small curtsy.

"How do you do," Mrs. Vanderpool said. "And what is your last name?"

"Lavin."

"Irish?"

"Yes, ma'am."

"Catholic?"

"Yes."

"You won't find any priests or nuns out here."

"No."

"Mother, James and I are very glad that Maggie and her sister have come to live with us and be our daughters. We need help, and I know Maggie is going to be a great help to me. I hope the dinner's to your liking. Come, Maggie!"

Maggie glanced at Mrs. Russell's face as they closed the door behind them. She's afraid of her, Maggie thought. And she realized that she, also, was a little afraid of the old woman whose eyes reminded Maggie of a hawk that Da had caught once when they were still in Ireland.

After the four sat down at the table, Mr. Russell said grace, thanking God for the food and for the daughters that He had sent them to help them and be a joy to them. Then, when he had finished grace he said, "My wife and I decided that we would have you call us Uncle James and Aunt Priscilla. We're not your parents, and I'm sure the words 'mother' and 'father' mean to you your own dear mother and father. But we can certainly be adopted uncle and aunt." He glanced at the two young faces in front of him. "Is that all right now?"

"Yes, Uncle James," they both said. Maggie smiled tentatively. Annie's eyes were on her plate, her fingers around her fork. "Can I start now?" she asked.

The Russells laughed together. "Eat!" they said.

Six

Maggie and Annie lay in the bed that had been built into the corner of the main cabin. At the other end were the embers of the fire.

After dinner the table had been pushed back against the wall, the silver and dishes washed in a bowl of warm water. Aunt Priscilla had shown them how to arrive at the right temperature by mixing water from the bucket with water from the kettle. When the dishes and silver were done, the water was poured outside and fresh water put in for the girls to wash before going to bed.

"Tomorrow," Uncle James had said, "I'll show you how to draw water from the well, and I'll take you both to the barn to meet the cow and her calf. Now go to sleep, both of you!"

Aunt Priscilla had kissed each good night. When she saw how torn Annie's nightgown was she said, "We'll have a sewing session, and I'll make you both new nightgowns and maybe a dress. Can you sew, Maggie?"

"No," Maggie admitted. There had never been time to learn, though she sometimes watched her mother doing it when Mrs. Lavin wasn't too worn out after her work.

"Never mind," Aunt Priscilla said, "I'll teach you."

Now Maggie lay on the outside of the bed, Annie between herself and the wall. Well, Ma, she thought. We're here. For so long, everything she had thought and done and made Annie do had been directed towards being here. Now they were here, in a home on the frontier. She felt she ought to feel satisfied, happy. Most of all, at home. But she didn't really feel that way. At least, not yet. It'll be all right, she told herself.

"What's that noise, Mag?"

Maggie pulled her mind away and listened. "I think it's the wind," she said.

"It sounds like a banshee."

"Now don't go getting imaginings." But, now that she was listening, she knew what Annie meant. The sound was like a queer, high howling.

"Does it always sound like that, Mag?"

"I don't know, Annie. Go to sleep."

It was barely light when Maggie woke up and became aware that Uncle James was building up the fire in the stove. When he had thrown some odd-shaped objects into it, he turned and glanced towards the bed. Maggie sat up.

"Time to get up," he said. "We start early here."

"What's that you're puttin' into the stove?" Maggie asked.

"Cow chips." He looked at her and smiled a little. "Dried cow manure. The plains have been an open range for years, first for buffalo, then for cattle, so there's plenty. It makes excellent fuel, and there isn't much wood around here."

"Are there buffaloes here then?"

"Once they covered the prairie. Now it's more cattle."

Maggie turned and poked Annie who didn't even stir. "Annie, Annie," she whispered. "Now wake up and get up. It's time."

Finally she just pulled her small sister to the edge of the bed and then off of it, forcing her to stand. Annie tried to get back under the blanket, but Maggie dragged her over to the bowl, wet Annie's washrag in cold water, and thrust it on her face. "Now wake up," she said.

Quickly they dressed. Maggie pulled on the loose-fitting dress the Children's Aid Society had given her before they left New York. It was a greenish black, but it was clean, and she had been told that she would grow into it.

Aunt Priscilla came in from the bedroom. "Good morning, Maggie. Good morning, Annie." She went to the windows and opened the shutters. "It's going to be a beautiful day."

"It's still dark," Annie said.

"Not really. Come over here, Annie. Let me show you that it really isn't still dark. Although I'm bound to say that two months from now it will be."

Annie went over to stand beside Aunt Priscilla and stood on tiptoe to see out the window.

"See?" Aunt Priscilla said. "This window faces the east, and you can see all that pink on the horizon. The sun is behind that, and soon it will come above the horizon and will shine gold, and it will be day. Here!" And Aunt Priscilla quickly stooped, put her arms around Annie's waist and lifted her up.

"It's pink!" Annie cried.

Aunt Priscilla laughed. "That's right."

"Put her down." Uncle James was standing in the doorway. "You know you shouldn't lift anything heavy."

"I'm not heavy," Annie said indignantly.

"I didn't mean you were. But your aunt has been ill and has been told not to lift anything heavier than a plate. That's one reason why you — and your sister — are here."

There was a short silence.

"Can I help you with anything?" Maggie asked.

"I'll show you how to make corn bread," Aunt Priscilla said. She took a heavy, flat, iron pan off the shelf. Maggie watched while she mixed cornmeal with water and salt in a bowl and shaped it into flat little patties. Then she put the patties onto the griddle. "Now watch these carefully, Maggie. Turn them once when they set around the edges and bubble in the middle. And while you're keeping an eye on those, please prepare Mother's tray. She'll have some special corn bread, which I'm heating up now, and scrambled eggs. The rest of us will also have bacon and potatoes, but she doesn't like either for breakfast. She'll have her coffee, of course."

How much food there was, Maggie thought, turning the patties, watching them brown, but in her mind seeing the empty cupboards in their apartment during the last months, the few pieces of stale bread there nibbled by mice and scurrying cockroaches. After Ma got sick

Maggie had cooked what food they had. She hadn't thought whether or not they liked it; it was simply a job to be done. Now, turning the patties, watching them get slowly darker, seemed oddly satisfying.

When Maggie started into Mrs. Vanderpool's room, Annie trailed after her until Uncle James said, in a sharper voice than Maggie had heard before, "No, Annie. Why don't you come over here and help Aunt Priscilla with the bacon?"

Quaking a little inside, Maggie pushed open the door next to the fireplace and went in.

As before, Mrs. Vanderpool was sitting up in bed, a fine red woollen shawl around her shoulders and underneath that a dark robe.

"It's usually done to knock," she said.

Maggie stopped. "I'm sorry. But with the tray it's hard to knock."

"Next time put the tray down and then knock and then pick it up again."

"Yes, ma'am." Maggie went over to the bed, trying not to think about the sickroom odor that was all too familiar. When she got the tray stationed on Mrs. Vanderpool's knees the old lady said, "You can take out the chamber pot now. Be sure it's properly rinsed and then bring it back. I never know when I'm going to need it."

Unlike the chamber pot that had been under her mother's bed, this didn't have a cover. Holding her breath Maggie walked out of the room with it and was making for the door when Annie ran towards her.

"No," Maggie cried, terrified that Annie would knock the pot out of her hands.

Mrs. Russell looked up from the stove.

"Oh — she shouldn't have asked you to do that now. I'm sorry. I'll take it for you." She started to come over.

"No, let Maggie do it," Uncle James said. "That is going to be one of her duties, and she may as well get started." He smiled. "You'll get used to it."

"Where do I empty it?" Maggie asked. She was trying not to breathe through her nose.

"I'll show you." Uncle James quickly opened the door and led the way around the back to the privy. "Empty it down the hole. There's some water there in the bucket you can rinse it out with. You'd better bring it back because she might need it. But you can empty yours after breakfast."

Maggie didn't look forward to going back into the room, but Aunt Priscilla was there and had opened the window a little. The air was fresher and smelled also of burned matches.

"You can sit down and tell me about yourself while I'm eating," Mrs. Vanderpool said.

"No, Mother," Aunt Priscilla said. "Maggie hasn't had her own breakfast. Go wash your hands, Maggie, and then sit down for grace. I'm sure you must be hungry."

Breakfast was delicious. Maggie and Annie had milk, cold from the barn, with their eggs, bacon, corn bread and browned potatoes. Maggie was full before she had finished all her potatoes.

"Clean plate now!" Uncle James said cheerfully.

Maggie, who was so full she could hardly breathe, slowly picked up her fork and speared a piece of potato. For a moment she held it in front of her mouth.

"You know," Aunt Priscilla said, "I'm hungrier than I thought I'd be. So if you don't mind, Maggie, I'll just take those potatoes off your plate because I didn't make any more." She turned to Annie. "Would you like some more potato?"

"Yes, please."

Uncle James laughed.

Aunt Priscilla put two small pieces of potato from Maggie's plate on Annie's, and the rest on her own. Annie ate the first of hers. Then she stared at the second. "I'm full."

"Well," Aunt Priscilla said, "I guess I'll just have to take it back. Now — "

"I'll give the extra pieces to Spot for now,"

Uncle James said. "Because I know you don't want it. And I don't want you to be sick by eating more than you want. But we can't afford to waste food here. When it's gone it's gone, and we can't go into town that often."

"I'm sorry," Maggie said.

"It's not your fault," Aunt Priscilla said. "We haven't had young ones around, and I forget that they don't eat as much. I'll give you a smaller helping next time. You can always ask for more."

"When you've finished with the dishes and the other chores," Uncle James said, getting up, "come out to the barn. I'll introduce you to the cow and the calf."

"Can I go out now?" Annie asked.

"No. You must stay and help your sister."

Maggie washed the dishes, and Annie dried them and put them on the shelf. Then they moved the table back and tidied up and smoothed the quilt on their bed.

Suddenly Mrs. Vanderpool's voice sounded from the next room. "I've finished with the tray. Somebody please come and get it. And I want to bathe."

Aunt Priscilla called in return, "Maggie will be with you in just a minute." Then she said to Annie. "Run out to the barn now, Annie, and get Uncle James to show you the cow and the calf."

When Annie had gone Aunt Priscilla wiped her hands and hung the towel on the metal rail beside the stove. Then she said, "Maggie, we . . . we decided to . . . to adopt a daughter to help me with Mother."

She hesitated. "Maybe I shouldn't say this because she is my mother, and of course I love her. But she isn't easy. She didn't want us — James and me — to come out here. And when she lost all her money and got so she couldn't live alone, she didn't want to leave Washington and come out here to be with us. But there was no other place she could go, and here she is. She hurt her leg and her hip badly, which is why she spends a lot of time in bed, and her heart isn't right."

Aunt Priscilla stopped and took a breath. "She's a proud woman, Maggie. Before the war she . . . well, she had a place in society. But a lot of her family were from the South. They were all but wiped out after the war. And with the change of things in Washington, she felt she didn't really have a place anymore. She's bitter. It won't be easy for you. I hope . . . I hope that you can do it without . . . well, just go along with what she says."

Maggie went into Mrs. Vanderpool's room.

The tray was pushed off her knees onto the side of the bed, and some of the coffee had tipped onto the tray and from there onto the quilt.

"You'll have to clean up that coffee. And I don't see why you couldn't have come in right away."

Maggie leaned over, straightened the cup, then carried the tray out.

"Everything all right?" Aunt Priscilla said.

"The coffee spilled a little on the quilt. Should I wash it with a wet cloth and soap?"

"It won't get it out, I'm afraid. But do your best. Here," and Aunt Priscilla handed Maggie a damp cloth. "I've soaped this part here, so you can try to clean it with that, and then rinse it off with the rest."

Maggie managed to get most of the coffee out.

"Now the quilt is wet on my legs," Mrs. Vanderpool said.

"I'll put a towel under it."

Helping Mrs. Vanderpool bathe took patience and skill. The old lady couldn't take any weight on her leg and hip. On the other hand, neither she nor Maggie wanted to risk getting the bed wet, so it was a question of Mrs. Vanderpool half standing and leaning on Maggie's shoulder while Maggie gave her a spot wash.

When Mrs. Vanderpool was finally back in

bed, she was tired. "I'll nap now," she said. "You can go."

Ma had always said "Thank you," Maggie thought, washing out the cloth she had used.

When she went back into the main part of the cabin, Aunt Priscilla said, "Why don't you go out to the barn now. You can meet the animals and maybe help Uncle James. I'm going to do a little sewing, and when you come back you can help me."

Maggie stood outside the cabin and stared at the waving grass of the prairie. For miles and miles there was nobody but themselves. She wondered how Lawrence was doing with the lawyer and his stout, kind-looking wife. In the lodging house in New York, some of the children had said they'd heard that orphans who'd been adopted had become like slaves. Maggie had pushed those words away from her. She told herself now that having to deal with Mrs. Vanderpool did not make her a slave. And Mrs. Russell — Aunt Priscilla — was as kind as she could be.

Then why, she thought, clutching her shawl, was she having a hard time not crying? Ma, she whispered in her mind. Ma.

The barn had a higher roof than the house did. Uncle James was using a fork to lift out the manure from the stalls of the cow and the calf, and those of the two horses, Rufus and Rumpkin. Annie was nowhere to be seen.

"Annie?" Maggie called.

"I'm up here!" And Annie suddenly materialized almost over Maggie's head. She was standing on a sort of balcony filled with hay. "There's a cat here," she said.

Uncle James looked up from the manure pile. "Annie, I told you to clean the harness."

"I'll do it," Maggie said quickly.

Uncle James looked at her for a moment. "Come and meet the cow. Have you ever milked a cow?" he asked.

"No."

"Well, it's never too early to learn. That can be one of your chores, which will free me for the planting and other outside work."

The cow was a big dun-colored animal. Beside her, the calf was the same buff-colored hue.

"Now," Uncle James said, pulling a three-legged stool over from the side of the stall. "Watch how I do this." He leaned down, took hold of one of the cow's teats in each hand, and pulled one after the other. Arcs of white milk squirted into the pan. He pulled a couple more times, then got up and said, "You try."

Maggie sat down on the stool, leaned over,

took hold of the cow's teats and pulled. No milk came out. The cow turned its head and made a funny noise.

Uncle James grinned. "She didn't like that."

Maggie was fighting an overwhelming desire to get up and leave. The cow was not friendly, and it was very large.

"Try again," Uncle James said.

Maggie pulled the teats again. A sharp pain ran up her back as something slammed into her. She jumped up, kicked the bucket over. "What happened?" Then she saw the milk trickling out onto the floor. "Oh — I didn't mean . . . I'll pick it up."

"She kicked you. That's what happened. Lucky for you there wasn't much in the bucket to begin with," Uncle James said. He picked up the bucket. "You're going to have to do better than that. Now put the stool up and try again. Only pull gently, sort of rubbing. Look, I'll show you again." And he took the teat and gently but firmly pulled it down. More milk squirted out.

"Can I try?"

They both turned. Annie was standing at the door, a ginger newborn kitten in her hand.

"No," Maggie said. "The cow will kick you."

"And put the kitten back," Uncle James said, "or the mother cat will scratch you." He turned

89

back to Maggie. "Now pull gently. I'll show you once more."

Once more the milk arced out. Once more Maggie sat down on the stool and took the teat in her hand. This time the cow's kick knocked her almost out of the stall.

She sat on the dirty floor, her back hunched, her arms hugging herself.

"You did it wrong," Annie said.

"I suppose you think you can do it better!" Maggie said angrily.

"No," Uncle James said. "I see now I expected too much of a city child."

Annie ran, put the stool up and sat down. Circling each hand around a teat, she gently but steadily pulled one. A little milk squirted out. The cow blew a bit, but didn't seem to mind. Annie pulled again, making a long continuous gesture of it. This time the arc of milk was fuller.

"I told you I could do it," Annie said.

Seven

Aunt Priscilla ran cold water over Maggie's back. "Cows can be contrary creatures. The one we had before this kicked James at least three times."

"I don't know what I did wrong," Maggie said. "I can see I wouldn't know it like Mr. R — Uncle James, but Annie did it right."

"It's possible Annie has a touch with animals. Some people do. Wasn't she talking of a little dog she once had?"

"Timmie," Maggie said gloomily. "It belonged to Mrs. O'Gorman who worked in the Green Harp, and who would let Annie look after him when she had to be behind the bar."

There was a short silence. Then Aunt Priscilla said, "I take it the Green Harp was a saloon — a place that sold alcoholic drinks."

"Yes. Me da used to go there." Maggie stopped. Angry and upset and in pain as she was, she couldn't go on to say that he had been in the Green Harp right before the boom on the ship killed him, and that maybe after more than a few beers, he wasn't paying the attention he should have been.

Aunt Priscilla took the cloth away for a moment or two. "This will probably help, but you're still going to have a bruise. I just hope it won't last too long."

"It'll be all right. I just don't know where Annie learned to do that. She never paid any attention to lessons or what people told her. I'd leave her to look after Ma, and then I'd find her playing with Timmie, and when I told her she should be at home with Ma, she said Ma'd gone to sleep."

"And had she?"

"Yes. But then she'd wake up again, and nobody'd be there."

"Annie's only seven. And you're a very responsible twelve. Maybe Annie saw somebody in New York milking a cow. People must drink milk there, so there had to be cows."

"There was a farm way up on Broadway that Ma used to go to sometimes, to get milk for us. But we both went with her, and I saw as much as Annie."

"I wouldn't worry about it. People have different abilities. My mother used to be able to play the piano beautifully, and she was never taught. She just listened to a tune and then could play it. I could never do that. But whenever Mother tries to cook, she burns something."

Uncle James tramped in. "That little girl seems to have some instinct about working with animals. It's amazing." He glanced at Maggie's back. "Ah well, maybe Annie can do the milking when I need help."

He picked up some tools from a shelf and walked out.

"You know, Maggie," Aunt Priscilla said, very gently drying Maggie's back. "I certainly don't believe in keeping anything important from someone you love, but perhaps I wouldn't mention the Green Harp to Uncle James. He's very strong for temperance, and one of the reasons he wanted to come out here and get away from the East Coast is that he felt people had a chance here to start over and prevent saloons and such like getting a hold in a new country."

"There'd be no reason for me to mention it," Maggie said, pulling her chemise over her back. "But there's no telling about what Annie'll say. She was powerful fond of Mrs. O'Gorman and silly about Timmie."

* * *

The bruise hurt Maggie badly for several days, but she was determined not to mention it. At night she would lie on the side away from the bruise, with her back to the outside of the bed so that Annie, who was a restless sleeper, wouldn't bump into it. The pain kept her awake for a while, but eventually exhaustion made her drop off, and she'd forget to keep her back to the outside of the bed. Then sometime in the night she would awake with a cry as Annie's arm, flung out, would hit the tender bruise. If it were near morning, she often did not go back to sleep.

The days started to develop a routine. Maggie would help Aunt Priscilla cook breakfast while Annie set the table. Then Maggie would take Mrs. Vanderpool's tray in, and she and Annie would wash up and tidy after the meal. Annie would go out to the stable, and Maggie would retrieve Mrs. Vanderpool's tray and help her get set for the day. This often took all morning, because Mrs. Vanderpool liked to be entertained, and sometimes demanded that Maggie talk to her.

Annie was kept well away from the difficult old lady.

After midday dinner Aunt Priscilla would go

out and work in her vegetable garden, although, as she told Maggie, there wasn't much to be done at this time of the year. Other times Aunt Priscilla would take up her sewing and would sit in the rocker that Uncle James had made for her and mend and sew.

The first thing from her skilled needle was a new nightgown for Annie, which had a small blue piping along the opening at the top.

"It was just a faded old blue dress that I only kept so I could use pieces of it," Aunt Priscilla said. But it made the nightgown into something pretty and special, because the blue brought out the blue in Annie's eyes. The first time Maggie saw Annie in it, her heart gave a painful jump. With her fair curls washed and dried by the fire, and the blue piping in the long gown, Annie looked like the popular idea of an angel. She also looked like Ma.

One night Maggie heard Annie singing to herself as they were about to go to sleep.

"What're you singing?" she asked Annie.

"I'm singing to Timmie," Annie said.

"Timmie's not here," Maggie said with a harshness that surprised her.

After that there was silence.

Maggie felt guilty about the way she had spoken. "What was the song?" she asked finally.

" 'The Wearin' o' the Green.' Mrs. O'Gorman

had me sing it at the Green Harp."

"Well, you'd best not be talking about it here," Maggie said. "Uncle James is very set against saloons and all that goes on in them."

Annie didn't say anything, but after a while she started singing again, very softly.

"How did you know how to milk the cow?" Maggie asked. It was a question that had been nagging at her.

"Don't you remember, Mag, when you and me and Ma went to the farm on Broadway? I watched the woman when she milked the cow, and Ma showed me afterwards with her hand how she used to do it in Ireland, kind of like stroking down."

Ma didn't tell me, Maggie thought. But then I didn't ask.

Saturday night at supper Uncle James said, "Tomorrow is the Sabbath. We go to church." He hesitated. "Did you go to church in New York?"

For a moment there was silence.

Then, "Yes," Maggie said briefly.

"I said lots of prayers to the Blessed Virgin," Annie added. "And Maggie and I went to Mass, didn't we, Mag?"

Uncle James cleared his throat. "Here we are Baptists and don't hold with the Blessed Virgin, and saints and Masses and all that flummery."

"But Ma's with the Blessed Virgin," Annie said. "I pray ten Hail Marys to her every night."

"That is nonsense!" Suddenly Uncle James's face was red. "The Blessed Virgin is no more — "

"James! Please let me speak." Aunt Priscilla was usually so quiet and gentle that the commanding note in her voice took everyone by surprise. Maggie saw Uncle James turn towards her, his face still red, his mouth a narrow line.

"I will not have — "

"These children were sent to us to help and give a home to. We knew they were Romans because the lady from the Society told us. And no matter what we think" — she said the words slowly and firmly — "we have no right to say belittling things about their parents' religion."

"Brother Evans said — "

"I don't care what the pastor said, James. We're supposed to be Christians."

"The Church of Rome is not — "

" 'Judge not that ye be not judged.' " Aunt Priscilla stood up. "That was said by an even higher authority than Brother Evans. Maggie, would you please go and get Mother's tray and see if there's anything else she wants?"

Uncle James took his coat and cap down from the peg on the wall and opened the door.

"Can I go and see the cow and calf?" Annie said.

"No!" he said and slammed the door.

Annie burst into tears.

"What was that all about?" Mrs. Vanderpool asked, when Maggie, first knocking, was told to come in.

"Uncle James doesn't like that Annie and I are Catholics."

She gave a cackle of laughter. "I bet he doesn't. He doesn't even like the fact that I've always been an Episcopalian and brought Priscilla up as one."

"What's an Episcopalian?" Maggie asked, lifting the tray off Mrs. Vanderpool's lap.

"My God! The ignorance of the Irish is boundless!"

Maggie stared at her for a moment, then let the tray fall back on Mrs. Vanderpool's knees. "I'll not listen to insults about the Irish!" she said, and walked out.

When she got out she went to Aunt Priscilla. An anger she didn't know she possessed was shaking her. Irish was Ma and Da. Irish was the sweet smell of the moor that she could sometimes remember. Irish was everything she was to her bones.

"I'll not be listenin' to insults about the Irish," she said to Aunt Priscilla. "Annie and me are Irish. We're proud of it. And it was the Protestants who took our land and burned our house and killed our animals." She felt suddenly an overwhelming need to be alone and snatched her shawl off one of the pegs. "I'm goin' out for a minute," she said, and went out, closing the door after her.

Mrs. Vanderpool's voice came loud and sharp from her room. "Send that girl back in here to get the tray. She needs a lesson in manners."

"Annie," Aunt Priscilla said in her normal voice, "just go on with drying the dishes. I'll be back in a minute." She went into her mother's room and closed the door behind her.

Annie, slowly wiping the dish that Aunt Priscilla handed to her, heard through the door the older woman's voice, strident and angry.

"I will not tolerate impertinence from some Irish — "

"Mother, keep your voice down!"

Annie heard that. Evidently it had some effect, because although Annie could hear the voices rising and falling, she didn't hear any more words.

Tears started to trickle down her cheeks. She was alone. Ma was dead. Timmie and Mrs. O'Gorman were days and days away. And now something terrible had happened to the Blessed Virgin. Uncle James would not allow her in the house.

The dish slipped out of Annie's hands, and she stood there, crying, staring at the pieces on the floor.

It was almost dark outside. The high grass was a line against the faint rose of the setting sun, a line that changed and moved. The sky to the east was black, and the stars hung there like diamond lanterns.

Funny, Maggie thought, she hadn't much noticed the stars in New York, but now that she thought about them, she knew that she saw them there, too, although they were farther away. Or perhaps it was because they were dimmed by the flaring torches and lamps on the street corners and shining from the houses.

There were always people about in New York: people leaning out the windows, on the steps of the houses, arguing in the streets, often yelling at one another. She'd hated it then.

When Ma had spoken of the rich with their haughty manners she had spoken also of their arrogant contempt for the Irish.

"They think we're stupid and common, Mag. I've seen their newspapers with pictures of the Irish made to look like monkeys, and in the grand houses, when we're standing there waiting on them at dinner, they talk about us as if we were deaf and couldn't hear and had no feelings."

And now she and Annie had come all the way across the country to this outlandish, deserted place to get away from all that only to find it again in the hateful old woman lying in her bed making belittling remarks about the Irish and ordering everybody about.

"I'll not stand for it," Maggie whispered to herself, and as she did so, tasted the tears that had flowed down her cheeks and onto her lips.

"And how're you going to stop them, Miss High-and-Mighty?"

The words and voice in her head were, strangely, those of Mrs. O'Gorman, although they could have been those of several of the neighbors on the street who thought Mrs. Lavin and her daughters were stuck up.

The truth was, Maggie couldn't stop them, and she knew it. There was nowhere she and Annie could go. People would be the same everywhere.

The last of the light slid behind the dark line

of the grass. Suddenly the world around her closed in. Behind her were the house, light flowing from the windows, and the barn, with its door open and lighted. Spot, always tied up now, could be heard snuffling around in his hut.

In the house was Mrs. Vanderpool. In the barn was Uncle James. Maggie stood there, hating to go into either, feeling the world hostile around her as she had never felt it before.

"Maggie?"

Maggie turned. Aunt Priscilla stood in the doorway of the house. Maggie knew that in the dark and as distant as she was from the house she wasn't visible. She could simply not answer and stay there.

"Maggie!" This time Aunt Priscilla's voice was louder. "Maggie, where are you? Where is Annie?"

Then Uncle James came to the barn door. "What are you talking about?" he asked his wife.

"Maggie and Annie are missing," Aunt Priscilla said.

"They're not in the barn." Uncle James started towards the house. Maggie, standing at a distance, half hidden by the outline of the outhouse, watched them both.

"What about the outhouse?" Uncle James

asked. He went to the outhouse door, knocked on it twice, then opened it. He struck a match and held it high. "Nobody here," he said. He turned to his wife. "You were in the house. What happened?"

"What happened was that Mother took up about the Irish where you left off about the Catholics. Between the two of you — and one was bad as the other — you must have made those two lonely, motherless children feel like unwanted outcasts."

By this time Uncle James had reached his wife, and they continued to talk, but Maggie couldn't hear. Besides, her anger had retreated before a fresh worry. "Where was Annie?" She shouldn't have walked out the way she had, she told herself, returning to the house. She should have remembered that she, not these people, was responsible for Annie, and that Annie often had no more sense than a goose. Thoroughly frightened now, she reached the front door and ran in. "Where is Annie?" she asked, as though she hadn't heard them a few minutes before.

"Where have you been?" Uncle James asked, anger in his voice. "You have no right — "

He stopped as his wife put her hand on his arm. "No, James. The wrong is the other way. I'm sorry, Maggie, for the things my mother said. She had no right to, and she has told me that she will apologize. I will take you in to see her. But first, do you know where Annie has gone?"

"No. What else was said that could drive her out?" Worry and anger made Maggie's voice sharp.

"Don't use that tone with your aunt," Uncle James said.

"Never mind that," Aunt Priscilla said. "I don't know of anything. I went in to talk to my mother about what she had said to you, and I closed the door so I don't think she could have heard anything that could have offended her. When I came out, I saw the plate here — " She pointed to three pieces on the table near the bowl.

"Broken," Uncle James said.

"Perhaps she thought you would beat her," Maggie said, not believing it herself.

"Would she think that, Maggie?" Aunt Priscilla's voice was firm but kind.

Maggie shook her head. "No. But she would have been that upset with what you said about the Blessed Virgin. She's always been a great one for the Blessed Virgin, and she thinks that Ma is with her, looking after us both from heaven."

Aunt Priscilla suddenly walked over to Maggie, put her arms around her, and kissed the top of her head. "We don't mean to be unkind," she said, her voice shaking a little. "And James, he isn't unkind, either. He's just like most men — his opinions sometimes get in the way of his good sense."

Once again Uncle James opened his mouth, then closed it. "I'm sorry," he said finally. "But do you think she just went out on the prairie?"

"I don't know. I'll go look for her."

"We'll all go. And let's call."

They all called, but there was no reply.

Finally Uncle James said, "You'd better go back now. If you go any further, you'll be lost, too. It's better I go on by myself." He looked at Maggie's face. "Don't worry. I'll find her."

When they got inside Aunt Priscilla said to Maggie, "Come with me." She led the way into her mother's room. "Now, did you have something you wanted to say to Maggie, Mother?"

Maggie saw the older woman's eyes on her.

"I have never in my life apologized to a child," Mrs. Vanderpool said, her haughtiness very much intact. "However, my daughter is right. I was rude. I apologize."

"Thank you," Maggie said coldly. And added, "Ma'am." She still hates us, Maggie thought. She's not sorry. But who's to take care of her if her daughter doesn't? She stared back at the dark eyes, giving hatred for hatred.

"I want you to go to bed, Maggie. I'm going to sit up. I have sewing to do, and I want Annie to see the light and come back in. I'm sure she can't be that far away. I just won't believe it."

"I'll sit up, too, Aunt Priscilla. I couldn't sleep anyway."

After a while, watching Aunt Priscilla put small, even stitches in a wide piece of cloth, Maggie said, "Do you think I could do that?"

"Of course. Would you like to? Here." Aunt Priscilla rummaged around her sewing box, found another needle, threaded it, and handed it to Maggie. "Now just watch me for a minute. I put the needle in here, taking up a small bit of both the cloth and the turnover, and then pull it through. Now you try on another side of the sheet." She watched while Maggie copied her. "That's very good! Are you sure you've never done it before?"

Maggie shook her head. Praise, rare in her life, made her want to cry.

"Well, just go on doing it that way until you get your side done. We'll finish the sheet in half the time."

Sick with worry as she was, Maggie found a peace in the rhythmic sewing. She had almost finished her side when she suddenly jumped up. "Of course. I'm daft. She'll be with the animals! Where's another light?"

Aunt Priscilla lighted another lantern, and they went quickly to the barn.

"I don't think she's here," Aunt Priscilla said a few minutes later.

But she was. Maggie, holding the lantern high, saw the edge of a boot and ran over to the hayloft. Curled around the mother cat and her kittens, Annie was asleep.

Eight

Maggie sat in the straight-backed wooden seat in the Baptist Church. On one side was Aunt Priscilla. On the other, Annie. Uncle James sat on the outside of the pew next to Aunt Priscilla.

The little church was packed. To Maggie it seemed a sea of bearded men, and women in sunbonnets. There were also children in almost every pew. Some turned around to stare at her and Annie, but were quickly made to turn back. The little girls wore sunbonnets, too. Maggie wondered if she and Annie would have to wear them. What they wore now were small straw hats given them by the Children's Aid Society, along with the dresses and coats that they now had on. Their fit left much to be desired. Nevertheless, they were moderately clean and warm, which, Maggie reminded herself, was more than could be said for the dresses they had left behind.

There were plain windows on the sides of the church, but Maggie was shocked to see there was no altar — just a huge pulpit on which rested the biggest Bible she had ever seen.

Even though they had started from the farm a full two hours before the ten-thirty morning worship service, they were still a little later than most of the rest of the congregation and swept in just as Brother Evans was announcing the opening hymn.

Aunt Priscilla had found the place for her in the big hymnbook and indicated that she was to share it with Annie.

It was a rousing hymn, and everyone sang loudly. Annie stood holding her half of the hymnbook, not making a sound, but as the second verse began, although she couldn't read the words of the hymn, she started singing wordlessly in a clear, high voice. But even with all the noise going on, Maggie had heard the whispered comments of the people across the aisle:

". . . the little orphans from New York I was telling you about."

"Shhhh, they'll hear you."

Maggie stared straight ahead, hearing Annie's treble rise above most of the voices around.

There was a long prayer said by Brother Evans who stood behind the lectern in the middle of the front of the church. For all his talk about miserable sinners and humble servants, Maggie thought, he addressed God as though he were telling Him exactly what to do and how to do it. Then Maggie jerked.

"And finally, God," the minister was shouting, "we ask You for Your mercy on those with us today who have been brought up in the ways of darkness, by people who knew not You, the One, True God. They are young, and it is not their fault," he added.

As if God didn't know young from old, Maggie thought furiously. For the first time she felt something like sympathy for Father O'Mara back in New York at St. Joseph's. But mostly she felt anger for the implied insult to Ma. Brought up in the ways of darkness, indeed! Her hands clenched in her lap, Maggie refused to incline her head during the prayer the way the others did.

Suddenly she was aware that Aunt Priscilla's hand, thin and worn, was resting lightly on her two. Her head was inclined, and her bonnet hid her face, but Maggie could feel her kindness and understanding as though she were talking. Maggie's hands unclenched.

The sermon was almost an hour long. Before it was half over Maggie became aware of Annie, fidgeting beside her.

"Shh," she whispered. "Be still now." She put out her hand and clasped Annie's, and held it that way until the sermon was over, squeezing it every time Annie showed signs of restlessness.

The minister shouted so much and talked in such a funny way that Maggie found it easy not to listen to him. Instead, she watched the sun come through the window and glance off his bald head. Instead of wearing the surplice and stole that Father O'Mara worn, he had on a dark suit with a stiff white collar and a black tie. Suddenly Maggie remembered the priest at St. Joseph's kissing the stole and putting it on before coming to hear confessions. It was so vivid that she wondered if Annie had had the same thought. She glanced down at her sister, and as she did Annie glanced up at her and smiled. Maggie put her arm around her and gave her a hug. At that moment she was intensely aware that they shared something no one else here had.

After the service they all filed out.

"So these are the two young 'uns from New York," someone from behind them said.

"Yes, these are our daughters," Aunt Priscilla stated. "Maggie, Annie, I want you to meet Mrs. Langdon."

Obediently they turned, and Maggie made a slight curtsy.

"You'll find things different out here," Mrs. Langdon said. She was a big woman in a gray dress that looked too tight and pulled in wrinkles under her arms.

"Yes, ma'am," Maggie said.

"I expect we'd find it different if we went to New York," another woman put in, coming around on the other side. She had on a black shawl over a rose dress, and her bonnet was rose-colored, too. She smiled. "I'm sure you'll have a wonderful time with the Russells. They're real good neighbors."

"Yes," Maggie said.

Finally they reached the back of the church.

"Brother Evans," Uncle James said to the minister, who was standing at the door of the church shaking people's hands as they left, "these are Maggie and Annie, our two girls from New York."

"May the Lord bless you," Brother Evans said, taking Maggie's hand in one of his and Annie's in the other. "As He already has by bringing you out of Sodom to these God-fearing parents."

112

"Ma was God-fearing, too," Maggie said.

"Yes," Aunt Priscilla agreed, "she was. Anyone that brought up two little girls so well and with such good feelings would have to be very God-fearing. And this is Brother Thomas, our assistant pastor," Aunt Priscilla said, introducing a young man with dark hair standing next to Brother Evans.

Maggie, expecting another Brother Evans, stiffened.

But Brother Thomas simply held out his hand, smiled shyly and said, "Welcome! We're glad you're here."

Uncle James and Aunt Priscilla introduced many of the people after that.

"What a pretty little girl," one woman said, looking at Annie.

"They're both pretty," her husband said.

"Pretty is as pretty does," another woman near them said sharply. She had been introduced as Mrs. Smiley, a former teacher at the school. Looking at Mrs. Smiley's narrow, tight mouth, Maggie smiled to herself at the absurdity of such a sour-looking woman having that name. But as her face relaxed into the smile, she saw the woman's eyes on her, and she hastily wiped the smile from her face.

They went into the room extending at a right angle to the main part of the church, where trestle tables had been set up and dinner was to be eaten before the afternoon Sunday school session. Everyone had brought food of some kind. Uncle James carried in a basket from the wagon, and Aunt Priscilla took out preserves, potato salad, bread, cheese, apples and pieces of fried chicken, which she put on big dishes in the middle of each table.

"That looks delicious," one woman said, eyeing the various dishes.

"Maggie helped me with the potato salad, the chicken and the bread," Aunt Priscilla said proudly.

Uncle James, hearing her, smiled a little.

Maggie, handing dishes from Aunt Priscilla to the women setting the table, saw how many children were there.

"This is my daughter, Jane," one woman said.

"How do you do," Maggie said formally.

"Hello," Jane said. She had a plain but good-natured face and straight brown hair in braids tied behind her neck. "How do you like it here?"

"Very much," Maggie said.

"Are you going to come to school?"

"I don't know. I guess so. Uncle James and Aunt Priscilla haven't mentioned it yet."

"There's our teacher over there. She's Miss Bailey and is real nice. But she's a one for spelling. Keeps you in if you don't learn."

Maggie's heart sank. Her schooling had been sketchy, partly because they had moved about and also because she had had to take care of Ma.

"You good at spellin'?" the girl asked.

"No," Maggie said.

"Hello, Jane," a boy said, coming up. He was tall and fair-haired. He looked at Maggie. "You one of the New York kids?"

"Yes."

"I'm Tom Brinton."

"Hello, Tom. This is Annie, my sister."

"Where?"

Maggie turned. Annie, who had been beside her five minutes before, had vanished.

"She was here a minute ago. Where could she have got to?" Maggie glanced hastily around the crowded hall. She could see no sign of Annie, but then Annie was so short she could easily be hidden by the full skirts and shawls. "I have to go and look for her," Maggie said.

"She'll be all right. She's probably just talkin' to somebody."

"No. I have to find her. She — I have to look for her."

"What can happen to her? She's perfectly safe here."

Maggie ignored him and started looking

115

among the people standing around.

"Maggie? Maggie?"

Maggie turned, recognizing Aunt Priscilla's voice.

"We still have work to do here, Maggie," Aunt Priscilla said.

Maggie was aware of the other women standing around. They had fallen silent, and though they were still moving around, putting things on the table, Maggie was aware they were listening.

"I — Annie's not here. I can't find her."

"Maybe she's gone to the privy at the back," one of the women said.

"Yes," Aunt Priscilla agreed. "Or she may just be outside enjoying the sunshine. Other of the smaller children are out there. Remember how anxious we were when she seemed to have disappeared before? And then it was dark. But she was in the barn all the time. Come along now, help me to put the milk in pitchers for each table, and then if she isn't back, we'll both go look."

Maggie knew Aunt Priscilla was appealing to her, and that she couldn't embarrass her by refusing to do as she asked. But everything in her screamed to find Annie immediately and keep her in her sight.

"Yes, ma'am," she said, and followed Aunt

Priscilla over to where the buckets of milk had been set by the door.

"You've been so responsible," Aunt Priscilla said, as she lowered the dipper into the milk and filled the pitchers. "You know now she's also my responsibility. I think you should be allowed to be a little girl yourself sometimes."

It was said in such a kind way, and the offer to take some of her burden was so well meant, Maggie couldn't understand her own reaction — a total rejection of the suggestion that Annie was anybody's responsibility but hers.

She swallowed. "Yes, ma'am," she said.

Maggie helped put the dishes on the table and napkins at each place. And she tried to make herself count the places at the two long tables. There were many of them. Memories of some of the nuns' teachings came to mind. It's like the feeding of the five thousand, she said to herself. But all she could think about was Annie.

Annie was safe here, the boy Tom Brinton had said. But he didn't know Annie and the trouble she could get into. He didn't know some of the things she'd done —

"Maggie, d'ye know there's a little doggie here that's a bit like Timmie."

Maggie turned around. Annie, her eyes shining and her cheeks red from the outside, was jumping up and down and grinning.

"You had no right to go outside without me," Maggie said. "Worrying me like that!" All her feelings for the past twenty minutes made her voice sharp.

Annie took a step back. "Yer didn't tell me not to."

"Why shouldn't she go out?" one of the women, the big one who had spoken to her upstairs, said. "My Jerry and Albert are out there, and so are lots of the other younger children. They're too young to be much good in here."

Uncle James was coming in with some of the men who had been talking outside. "What's the matter now, Maggie?"

"Nothing," Maggie said. She knew that with these people she was in the wrong. They don't understand, she told herself.

Uncle James looked at her for a moment, then turned to Annie. "So, you like Dr. Prendergast's little dog, do you?"

"He's like Timmie, Mrs. O'Gorman's little dog that I took care of, 'cept Timmie was a bit browner. What's his name, Uncle James?"

Uncle James glanced at the big fair man who was listening to the conversation with a smile. "Well, Will, what's your dog named?"

"His name is Runt, because he was the runt of the litter. Did you like him?"

"Yes. Can I go out and play with him again?"

"We'll be eating any minute now, Annie," Aunt Priscilla said. "You can go out afterwards, or perhaps after Sunday school, and play with him a bit. That is if Dr. Prendergast doesn't mind."

"I don't mind at all. Come and tell me about Timmie, Annie."

Maggie suddenly remembered Aunt Priscilla's suggestion that Mrs. O'Gorman, and most of all, the Green Harp, should not be mentioned before her husband.

"Annie," she said. "Come and help me with the milk here."

"Nonsense," Uncle James said. "Go along and tell Dr. Prendergast about Timmie. She has a feeling for animals," he added to his friend. "She milked old Bess first try. Maggie here couldn't manage it at all."

"But Maggie sewed a beautiful seam in our new sheet, James. I've never seen a better," Aunt Priscilla said. Evidently the same thought about Mrs. O'Gorman and the Green Harp had struck her. "Let Annie help Maggie with — "

But it was too late. Annie was well away in her story. "And whenever Mrs. O'Gorman went to work at the Green Harp, she'd send me a message to come take Timmie out and play with him. He was that good with bringing back sticks, and he always minded me as well as he did Mrs. O'Gorman. There were times when she came back to her house after being long at the tap and not too steady in her walk — "

"What did you say?" Brother Evans turned from the door and asked in a stern voice. "Already the devil and his works — "

"That is nonsense, Brother Evans. Annie is just a baby," Aunt Priscilla said. "And we have to remember she and her sister were sent here by the Society to get them away from harm. I will not have them publicly scolded like this, as though they had done wrong."

"But — "

"Don't be an idiot, Evans." Dr. Prendergast stared down the shorter preacher. "And don't start throwing sins around among youngsters that don't even know what the sins are. That's not God's work."

"The devil — " the preacher started.

" 'Suffer little children to come unto me,' " a gentle-voiced woman from the back said. "We all know who said that."

"Taught by heathen parents!" Brother Evans muttered.

Annie ran up to him and beat on him with her fists. "Ma is with the Blessed Virgin," she said, and burst into tears.

Nine

The fuss about the Blessed Virgin clattered on. Voices got louder. Dr. Prendergast stated that he, for one, would not come back to the church until Brother Evans promised he would stop picking on the two New York children.

Maggie, clasping Annie by the hand, had stood there while the adults talked and argued. It seemed that everyone had forgotten about them, and had also forgotten about fixing lunch. Maggie felt more torn than she ever had before.

Kansas was not like New York. The people here were cleaner. They did not get drunk and brawl. For all the unpleasantness connected with nursing Mrs. Vanderpool, the house was sparkling clean, the food was delicious, for the first time in their lives she and Annie didn't have to worry about getting enough to eat, and they were not in constant danger of being evicted by the landlord for not paying the rent — a fear that haunted their years in New York.

But — it was the "but" that was making her feel so torn. At home everybody they knew were Catholics. The grand people were Protestants, of course, but they weren't friends, just employers. She wondered what Ma would think of Brother Evans. And then, as clear as though Ma were in her mind, talking, she heard her say, "Ach, Maggie, they're all alike — he's no better than a priest! Pay no attention!"

At that moment she remembered what Aunt Priscilla had said about Uncle James, that he wasn't unkind, just that he was like most men: "his opinions get in the way of his good sense." Recalling that, her heart lifted a little. Ma was Ma and was special. But Aunt Priscilla was kind and nice.

"Hi."

Maggie turned. Tom Brinton was there.

"Lunch ought to be ready pretty soon," he said.

"Maybe they won't let Annie and me eat with you, seeing as how we're heathens and brought up in darkness."

122

He grinned. "That's just Brother Evans and one or two others. They'll calm down in a minute. There are some ducks in the pond outside. They just came in, on their way south. Want to go and look at them?"

Tom, Maggie and Annie walked out to the pond and looked at the beautiful birds. Some of them had necks and heads of a dark blue-green. Others were brown and speckled.

"Which ones are the blue?" Maggie asked Tom.

"The drakes." He looked at her and smiled. "The males. The females are the brown ones."

"The drakes are so much prettier," she said. "It doesn't seem fair."

Annie bent and dabbled in the water. She had cried for a while after being reproved for beating on Brother Evans, and her face was smudged.

"Come here, Annie. Your face is dirty." Leaning down, Maggie put a corner of her handkerchief in the water, then straightened and started trying to clean Annie's face.

"She *is* with the Blessed Virgin," Annie said and hiccoughed.

"You can think she's wherever you want," Tom said. "I just wouldn't talk about it. All you'll get is trouble!"

"I know she is," Annie said, and started

crying again. "She promised she would be."

"Annie, luv, now stop crying," Maggie wiped away at the smears. "You and I and the holy saints know she's with the Blessed Virgin. What does it matter what a bunch of Protestants think?"

"That's right," Tom said.

Maggie realized as she spoke that she was undercutting all her previous efforts to make Annie think they'd be better off here. But she hadn't expected all this trouble about religion. Somehow she had always thought that out here it would be different. "It's a pity people have to have opinions. They'd be much better off without them," she said.

"But you have to have opinions, Maggie," Tom protested. "I mean, about things like right and wrong."

"And where do they get you? Mind, I'm not talking about stealin' and hurtin' somebody. Everybody knows that's wrong. But all those people in there, still blathering about the Blessed Virgin and Ma! They don't know a thing. They upset Annie, and they think that's all right. But she says Ma's with the Blessed Virgin — and who's to say she is or isn't — and they haven't stopped talking." She paused. "Uncle James will be upset." When she said that she knew she was afraid.

"Aw, you'll see! They'll have a big chinwag, and then they'll settle down."

And it seemed he was right. After a few more minutes, Aunt Priscilla and Uncle James came out to the pond. "Come along, now, children," Uncle James said. "Time to have dinner and then Sunday school."

And an hour later, there they all sat peacefully, listening to the story of Saul and David as though nothing had happened. Or almost nothing. Maggie, eyes rigidly ahead, was aware of glances thrown in her direction.

She thought Annie was beside her until something made her turn her head, and she saw Uncle James sitting on a bench towards the back, Annie on his lap. Maggie was glad, of course, that he was fond of her little sister. But it somehow made her feel lonely.

Just as they were about to get in the wagon after Sunday school, Dr. Prendergast strolled over. Runt was with him, running around and smelling things.

"Runt!" Annie cried.

The little dog put up his head and then trotted over, his tail erect, his ears up.

As Annie patted him, his ears came down, and his whole backside wagged back and forth with pleasure. "Good Runt," she said. Picking up a stick lying near, she threw it. Runt took off and retrieved the stick, bringing it back proudly.

"He brought it back, Uncle James. See, he brought it back!"

"I do see, Annie. But right now I'm going to put you in the wagon. It'll be dark by the time we get back. Come on, now!" And he heaved her up over the side. "Maggie?" he said.

Maggie had already learned the technique of putting her foot on the hub of the wheel and then swinging her other leg over. "I can manage," she said.

Tom Brinton was standing by. "Coming next Sunday?" he asked.

Maggie looked at Aunt Priscilla, sitting up next to the driver's seat.

"Yes, she is," Aunt Priscilla said. "And what's more, she'll be in school this week."

"Some of the time, anyway," Uncle James said. "Let's go!"

As they were driving back, Annie turned and said to Uncle James's back, "I never see Spot. Don't you have him anymore?"

"Yes, but I've been keeping him tied up behind the barn so he wouldn't frighten you two children."

"He must be lonely," Aunt Priscilla said.

"You used to let him come into the house sometimes, and he liked lying in front of the fire."

"You wouldn't be happy if he attacked Maggie or Annie," Uncle James said. "He's a guard dog, and you can't have it both ways."

"Maybe if you went up with each child to him," Aunt Priscilla said. "We'd do that with dogs at home when somebody new joined the family."

"Did you have dogs, Aunt Priscilla?" Annie asked. She got to her feet so she was standing right behind Aunt Priscilla.

"Sit down, honey, or you'll fall. Yes, we had dogs, mostly hunting dogs."

"They were dogs for pleasure, not for guarding," Uncle James said rather severely.

"Now, James, that isn't fair. They were working dogs. They earned their keep. In the hunting season they ran miles."

"I wouldn't know about such rich ways of living."

There was something about his voice that ended the conversation.

When they reached home Uncle James went to the pot that was on the stove, lifted the lid and put some of the contents into a dish. "Maggie, Annie, I'm going out to feed Spot. If

I'm to introduce you, I think this is the best way to do it."

Maggie considered Spot a squat, ugly dog and had no particular desire to know him any better. However, she did not want to have to deal with him by herself if no one else was around, so she went along with Annie who was skipping and hopping at Uncle James's side.

Spot's shed was on the other side of the barn. He had been barking when they got home, then quieted, now barked again. Maggie felt fear lick up her body. Since he was tied up behind the barn, she hadn't seen him since their arrival, but she remembered the savage growl in his throat and the thrust of his blunt muzzle with the little eyes above it.

"Now, Spot," Uncle James said. "I want you to meet new family members." He went up to the dog who was barking frantically and patted its head.

To Maggie's surprise, the savage brute stopped barking, wagged its stump of a tail and jumped up and tried to lick Uncle James's face.

"All right, all right! Annie, I want you to come here."

Annie, who had been excitedly jumping around ran obediently over. Maggie watched Uncle James's hand, holding Spot's collar.

"Don't come too fast," he said abruptly. "Just walk slowly."

Annie stopped, then walked slowly forward.

"Now," Uncle James said. "Put your hand out like this." And he thrust out his other hand, palm down, holding it steady. "Put your hand about this far from Spot."

Maggie watched fascinated as, without fear, Annie put her hand exactly where he had told her. Spot strained forward. Uncle James let him approach her hand and sniff it. Then Spot sniffed her arm, her clothes, her shoes, and back to her hands. Without being told Annie turned her palm and patted him on the head. His ears went down. He stood there. After a minute he wagged his tail.

"He likes me," Annie said.

Uncle James gave one of his rare but attractive laughs. "I think you're right. But that's not hard to figure. You're all set to like him, aren't you?"

"Yes," Annie said delightedly.

"All right. Now you go on standing there. Maggie, you come forward slowly."

For a second Maggie hesitated. She wanted to go back to the house. In that second Uncle James looked up, and Maggie knew that he could see she was afraid.

"It's all right," he said gently. "I have him. He won't get loose."

Maggie was furious that he had seen her afraid. Lifting her head up she started walking briskly towards the dog.

"Slowly," Uncle James said.

She let herself slow down. Step by step she followed what Annie had done, and when Spot had sniffed at her hand, arm, clothes, shoes and then her hand again, she forced herself to turn her hand and pat him.

Spot growled. She jumped back.

"Now stop that!" Uncle James cuffed the dog. He looked up at her. "I guess he knows you're scared. Go back and bring his dish. That ought to make him like you."

Maggie went back and picked up the full dish from where Uncle James had put it down. When she placed it in front of Spot, and Uncle James let him loose, he thrust his huge muzzle into the dish and started gobbling down the food. Annie bent down and started stroking him.

"I wouldn't interfere with him while he's eating," Uncle James said. And then laughed again. "I guess he doesn't mind with you." Because though Spot went on eating voraciously, his backside wagged as she patted his head.

"Okay, girls, go back to the house. I'm going

to loose Spot. Priscilla is right, it's not fair or right to the dog to keep him tied up all the time like that."

Maggie took Mrs. Vanderpool's supper tray in. It was their first meeting since the old lady had apologized to her. Maggie was determined to be polite so there could be no reproach to her. But she was also determined not to give an inch. She would give hatred for hatred.

But Mrs. Vanderpool seemed to be in a good mood.

"How did you like church?" she asked, and then, when Maggie stiffened, said, "I was not making a . . . a controversial remark. It was just a casual question, so don't get your haughty back up."

Maggie turned towards her, tray in hand.

There was a sparkle of humor in the woman's eyes. "Well, are you going to pretend to me that you don't have stiff-necked pride? I saw the way you pokered up."

"It was all right," Maggie said. And then, "They don't have incense."

"No. But they do have sermons that last an hour." She looked quizzically at Maggie. "Don't tell me you didn't notice it."

Maggie grinned a little. "It was long."

"Did it come out that you were Catholics?"

"Yes. Annie told Brother Evans that Ma was with the Blessed Virgin."

To Maggie's surprise, Mrs. Vanderpool put her head back and laughed. "I'll bet he loved that!"

When supper was over, and everything cleaned up, and Mrs. Vanderpool settled for the night, Aunt Priscilla called Maggie over to where she was wiping off some dishes.

"Maggie, dear, how much schooling did you have in New York?"

"Not . . . not much. I learned some letters and can read some, but not everything."

"And Annie?"

Maggie shook her head. "She learned a few things from the nuns at church, but she can't read."

Aunt Priscilla hesitated. "I don't want you to have a difficult time at the school here. I thought at first that I'd teach you myself to read before we let you go there, but James said we promised the Children's Aid Society that we'd send you, so we will. When . . . if Mother needs extra care sometimes, then maybe you will occasionally have to stay home a day or two." She paused. "I hope that won't happen too often."

Ten

Uncle James drove them to school after breakfast. It had been a rushed morning. Mrs. Vanderpool was not fully awake when Maggie carried her tray in, and grumbled that she didn't like getting up that early.

When Uncle James rose up from the breakfast table and said, "All right, girls, time for school," Maggie had said to Aunt Priscilla, "I haven't taken Mrs. Vanderpool's tray out yet, or tidied her." "Tidying" was a term that covered emptying her chamber pot, helping her bathe and straightening her bed.

"That's all right. I'll do it after I finish the dishes. Here are your lunches." And she handed Maggie and Annie each a brown paper package tied with string.

There was a sharp edge to the air and a

leaden look to the early morning sky. Uncle James sniffed as he drove Rufus and Rumpkin on the path through the ploughed fields and then through the prairie grass. "We could have snow before nightfall," he said.

"I could make a snowman," Annie said. "I once made a snowman in front of Mrs. O'Gorman's house, but some big boys came and knocked it down."

"That wasn't very nice. I don't think anyone would knock your snowman down here in Kansas," Uncle James said.

The two girls were up on the seat with him, Annie huddled between Maggie and Uncle James. Maggie had a great desire to say, "Only if it was a Catholic snowman," but she didn't allow herself to speak.

"Are you warm enough?" she finally asked Annie.

Aunt Priscilla was busy making two linsey-woolsey dresses for the girls, but with everything she had to do, it was slow work, and in the meantime all each had was the cotton dress supplied by the Society.

"I'm fine, Mag," Annie replied.

It was a puzzle to Maggie that Annie never seemed to feel cold any more than she felt dirt.

"I can give you my shawl if you're not."

"You're a born mother, Maggie," Uncle

James said. The way he said it, the tone in his voice, filled Maggie with pleasure. Then, "Don't get too happy," she told herself. It was an old reflex reaction. "Ah, Maggie," Ma had said more than once, "enjoy things as they come. Ye'll never be happy if you don't." And what had being happy in the moment brought Ma except illness and death? Maggie wondered, staring into the grayness and feeling the sharp wind on her face. She knew that thinking the way she did was wrong, that Ma would have said it was wrong, yet she couldn't stop herself.

The school sat at the top of a low hill with a few trees dotted around. It was a square building made of logs with a peaked roof and, at one end, a small bell tower sheltered by a little roof of its own. The children hadn't gone in yet, and were playing and shouting outside.

"All right now," Uncle James said, tying the horses' reins to a post, "I'll take you over to meet Miss Bailey." Then, "When school's over, you know the way back, don't you, Maggie?"

"Yes. Just follow that path through the grass and then through the fields."

"It shouldn't take you more than half an hour. And the McCandless children will be coming part of the way with you. The path leading to their house branches off near that little cluster of oaks I showed you — about halfway home."

"I'm so glad to see you," Miss Bailey said when they walked up, and Uncle James introduced them. She was the tall young woman Jane had pointed out in the church hall. She was bareheaded, and her auburn hair was caught up at the back in a big knot. "I'm sure you'll have lots of interesting things to tell us about New York."

After Uncle James had gone, Miss Bailey checked the watch that hung from a pin on her shoulder and said to Annie, "Would you like to come in and help me ring the bell?"

Annie, who had been extremely quiet, gave a little hop and grinned. "Yes," she said. They went off together into the school.

When the bell rang Maggie joined the other children who streamed into the school. Not knowing where to sit she hesitated, standing just inside the door, watching the other children come in and go straight to their seats.

She counted forty-nine sitting at desks in two sections of five rows each. In one section sat boys; in the other across the aisle, girls. The youngest were in the front, the oldest in the back rows. Maggie recognized many of the children from church and Sunday school the day before.

In the front area behind the teacher, there was a stove to one side, a blackboard on an easel, and a chair and desk.

Miss Bailey was standing at the front holding Annie's hand. She looked over the heads of those at their desks to Maggie. "Maggie, come over here and join Annie and me. I want to introduce you both to the school."

Maggie walked to the front and stood with Miss Bailey and Annie.

"Girls, boys, I want you to welcome Maggie Lavin and her younger sister, Annie Lavin. They're from New York and they're going to live with Mr. and Mrs. Russell."

There was a silence. Finally one older girl at the back said, "Hello." To Maggie she sounded polite, but not welcoming.

Then Maggie noticed Tom Brinton, seated in the fourth row of the boys' section.

"Hi," he said, and smiled.

Another boy, sitting near the back, leaned out of his desk and said, "Are you the Catholics?"

"Yes," Maggie said.

"What if they are?" Tom said.

"Exactly, Tom," Miss Bailey agreed. "The

main thing is that they are going to be part of our school."

A very pretty girl sitting in the third row said, "Ma doesn't think we should associate with Catholics."

"Well, my ma didn't think much of Protestants," Maggie flashed.

"Stop it, both of you!" Miss Bailey said. She paused. "I hoped very much this wouldn't happen. And I am ashamed of you, Ellen. As far as I am concerned, your attitude is un-Christian, and if your mother wants to talk to me about it, I'll be happy to go into it with her. This is a country founded by people who had been persecuted for their religious beliefs. We don't want to do to anyone what was done to us, now do we?"

Ellen looked down, but Maggie noticed that she also glanced sideways at Tom.

Miss Bailey paused a moment. "I think we could all learn a lesson from this today. Maggie, could you tell us a little about what took your family from Ireland — did they suffer while they were there?"

Maggie was taken aback. What had happened to the Lavins and many of their Irish friends and neighbors in New York was something they grumbled about among themselves. Still, she'd spoken about it to Aunt Priscilla. She took a breath.

"We — me da and ma and I — lived in a cottage on the estate of an English lord. There used to be more cottages, but the people died from the famine, the potato famine. Anyway, the lord's agent — we never saw the lord himself — came and told us that we had to leave because the lord wanted the land to graze his horses. Me da said we'd been in the cottage all his life, and his father's and grandfather's lives, and we weren't leaving. So the agent came in the night and set fire to the house and the barn, killing our animals. There was nowhere for us to go. So we finally got passage to America."

"You see," Miss Bailey said, "what some people suffered before coming over."

"Wasn't it your house?" The question came from the boy who had asked if they were the Catholics.

"No," Maggie said, shocked that he could be so ignorant. "And where would we get the money? Anyway, the owners have no right to turn the people off the land. They work for the owner who gets their crop money, and he's supposed to look after them."

"Sounds a funny way to do things to me," another boy said.

"I think it's terrible," a girl in the second row spoke up. "I've heard about that kind of thing. Tenant farming, it's called. I'm glad Maggie and Annie are here. I hope they'll be happy."

As though this had released something, there were murmurs of agreement. Maggie felt something hard and tense in her relax.

The pretty girl combed her fingers through her curls. "Well, if you came to this country to do better, why did you have to be sent out here as orphans? Was your family too poor to look after you properly?" The tone cut more than the words.

There were two or three sniggers.

Maggie could feel her face burning. Annie suddenly let go of Miss Bailey's hand and ran around to Maggie. Clutching and grabbing at her hand, she said, "I want to go home now, Mag. Let's go."

Maggie could tell she was near tears. "It's all right, Annie," she said. She knew that though Annie throughout her short life had lived in poverty and squalor and had been exposed to disease and had often been hungry and had few clothes, she had never really encountered what was now facing her and Maggie: active hostility.

"It's all right," Maggie said again loudly. "There are mean people everywhere. It's best to ignore them."

"I apologize to you and Annie for what was just said," Miss Bailey said. "Ellen, I want you to come and sit in the front of the room among the young children. When you go home I'll send a note to your mother. Now please do as I say!"

"I'm not going to sit among the babies," Ellen said, her hand going through her curls. "Just because — "

"At once!" Miss Bailey said.

The pretty girl finally stood up, picked up her books and flounced to the front of the room.

"And you will sit there until you apologize to Maggie and Annie," Miss Bailey said. She looked around the room. "Mary Prendergast?" she said.

One of the smaller girls seated near the front stood up. "Yes, Miss Bailey?"

"I want you to share your desk with Annie here. There isn't anybody in the other half, is there? I know that Sue and Myrtle are not here today, but neither of them sits with you, does she?"

"No, Miss Bailey."

"Well, why don't you come here and accompany Annie back to your desk so she'll feel at home."

"I want to go home," Annie said, clinging to Maggie's hand.

"No, Annie," Maggie said. "We have to stay here. Go with Mary."

But Annie hung onto Maggie's hand until Mary, a plump, good-natured-looking child, came up and said, "Mama gave me some cookies for lunch. You can have one if you like."

"Don't turn her down," Tom said. "She hasn't offered anyone else one."

Mary held out her hand, and Annie finally let go of Maggie and put her hand in Mary's. As they walked back Annie said, "Do you live with Runt?"

Everybody laughed, but in a kind way.

"Yes," Mary said, showing Annie to the seat inside. "But he likes Daddy best. I have Chicago."

"Is Chicago a dog like Runt?"

"No, Chicago is a cat. I named him Chicago because that's where we all came from. Everybody thinks I'm crazy to have Chicago with me in my room at night instead of letting him be in the barn where he can catch mice, but I don't see why he has to be out there. It's cold."

"And he'd get more to eat with you, wouldn't he?" a red-headed boy said, grinning.

"Be quiet, Harry," Mary said. And then to Annie, "That's my brother Harry. He's jealous."

"Who'd be jealous of an old cat?" Harry said.

Mary put out her tongue at him.

Maggie, standing up at the front beside Miss Bailey, felt the teacher tense at her side. Everybody quieted, waiting to see what the teacher was going to do about Mary.

Miss Bailey sighed. "That's not the best way to convey your feelings, Mary. But in honor of Annie and Maggie, I'll pretend I didn't see." She glanced over the room. "Maggie, there doesn't seem to be a place on the girls' side, so I'm going to do an unprecedented thing. I'm going to put you temporarily on the boys'. Tom, you seem to be occupying a double desk by yourself. Would you let Maggie share it with you?"

Tom got up and made an elaborate bow. "I'd be elevated."

"I'm not sure that that's quite what you had in mind. I think you meant honored."

"Okay, honored. Come on, Maggie. Come sit here."

Maggie, feeling better than she could have thought possible ten minutes before, walked back to where Tom was now sitting.

"Welcome," Tom said.

Maggie could feel herself blushing. She always had a harder time responding to people being nice than to people being unpleasant. "Thank you," she said.

Just as she sat down she encountered Ellen's eyes — dark and hostile. She likes Tom, Maggie thought. And Tom likes me. It made her feel warm and a little powerful.

As Maggie looked at the reader Miss Bailey handed her she knew that she wasn't able to follow more than a few words. Again, color burned in her cheeks. If the teacher got to know that, Maggie, too, would be put among the young children, only not for being rude, but for ignorance, which was so much worse. As Miss Bailey called on one child after another to stand up and read, Maggie sat there, growing sick with dread that her name would be next. But the morning passed, and the teacher did not call her name.

At twelve Miss Bailey rang a handbell. "Lunchtime," she announced. "Maggie, I'd like you to come up here for a minute or two."

While the other children ran out into the fresh air, chattering, Maggie went up to Miss Bailey's desk. Annie, she noticed, ran out with Mary Prendergast. She seemed quite happy.

"How much schooling did you get, Maggie?" Miss Bailey asked gently.

"Not much. I had to take care of Ma. She was sick off and on before she died. She wanted us to go," Maggie added hastily, "but with her being in bed and all, I had to do things for her and to watch after Annie. Sometimes the nuns — " She stopped. Nuns were probably on the disapproved list, too.

144

Miss Bailey reached in her desk drawer and took out the reader that Maggie had looked at with Tom. "Can you read this?" she asked, pointing to a page.

Maggie looked at it and shook her head. At that moment she caught sight of Ellen, loitering around the doorway. She glanced up. Miss Bailey, seeing her, looked also.

"Ellen, please go outside and keep an eye on the young children. Now!"

Ellen tossed her curls back and moved away from the doorway.

"Can you read any of the words at all?" Miss Bailey asked in a lower voice than she usually used.

Maggie pointed to short words in the text. "The, and, to, but, dog, tree," she said.

The teacher didn't say anything for a moment. Then, "I'm going to write a note to Mrs. Russell. She was a teacher, you know, and I'm going to suggest that she help you a little so that you won't feel so behind others of your own age. I know she'll do it; she's one of the nicest people I know." The teacher glanced up. "Don't you think so?"

"Yes," Maggie said. It was wonderful to be able to say this with honesty. "She's kind."

"Now, does your sister have any words she can read?"

Maggie shook her head. "No. Mind, she

draws pictures. Of course, the nuns weren't keen on that."

Miss Bailey smiled. "Why?"

"Well she's daft about dogs, so she drew dogs. They were supposed to be Timmie, the little dog she looked after sometimes."

"Maybe I'll ask her to draw a dog. But it won't be so bad if she can't read. Others of her age in school can't. They don't all start at the same time. By the way, how are you going home? Is Mr. Russell coming after you?"

"No. He said we could just follow the path and walk, that there was a family that lived near us, and we could go with them."

Miss Bailey was silent for a minute. Then she said, "That's true, the McCandless sisters, Ellen and Hannah, do live near you. So I suppose you'll go with them."

Eleven

"Is that the kind of hat they wear in New York?" Ellen asked, as she and Maggie, Hannah and Annie trudged along the path through the grass. The snow that Mr. Russell predicted was beginning to come down slowly in widely spaced flakes.

"Yes," Maggie said. She drew the big shawl around her and glanced at Annie. Annie's hat, which had shabby ribbons tied in a bow under the chin, was on backwards. If Maggie had been with Annie when she put on her coat and hat that wouldn't have happened, but they were at opposite ends of the schoolroom, and Tom Brinton had delayed her to say that he was glad she'd come to school, and if there was anything he could do, he'd be happy to help her. And Ellen McCandless had been within earshot when he'd said that. Maggie hunched her shoulders a little. She knew it would not be a comfortable walk. But she and Annie needed someone to show them the way, at least this first time.

"That's funny," Ellen said. "Mama gets magazines from New York and Boston. They show the latest fashions, and hats like that went out years ago."

"We didn't have money to buy new hats all the time," Maggie said. She knew she was being baited, and hotter retorts than that sprang to her tongue. But at this moment, with the snow coming down, she needed Ellen.

"Anyway," Annie suddenly said, "the ladies at the Society gave us these hats, didn't they, Mag?"

"What society?" Ellen asked. Then before Maggie could answer, she said, "You mean one of those charitable societies that Grandmother has told us about? Grandmother came from Baltimore, you know. She said all the ladies used to give out food and clothing to the poor. I guess that meant you, didn't it?"

"Do you have to be so mean, Ellie?" Hannah said. She was about ten and rather plain.

Ellen giggled. "Am I being mean? I'm so sorry. We haven't had charity people around here before, so I guess I don't know how to act."

Suddenly, and before anyone could stop her, Annie went up and kicked her in the shins. "Pig, pig, pig," she yelled.

"Why you — " Ellen aimed a slap at her, but was foiled by Maggie who was thinner than Ellen but a little taller. Maggie caught her arm and held it. "If you hit my sister you'll be sorry!"

"She kicked me!"

"You deserved it!"

"She's only being mean because Tom Brinton likes you," Hannah said. "She's had a crush on him all year."

Ellen turned on her sister. "If you say anything more, I'll tell how you stole some of the cookies Mama made before she could give them to Mrs. Pearson, and then when she asked you, you lied about it."

Hannah's eyes filled with tears. "I only took them because you took half of mine."

"And I told you, when you told Mama that, she asked me, and I told her it wasn't true, and she believed me, not you, so there!"

Hostilities ceased as abruptly as they had began. Annie had left Hannah's side and was now holding Maggie's hand as they trudged through the snow. The flakes were falling faster. It was becoming harder to see the trail.

If they hadn't had such a fight Maggie would have asked how much further lay the fork where they branched off. But she couldn't bring herself to ask anything. The snow was coming through her shawl and wetting her dress. She glanced quickly at Annie. Her hat was now mostly over one ear. Her fair hair was dark with wet and her old, worn coat was showing large damp spots. Maggie felt that if she had any idea how much longer it would take to get to the Russells' it would be easier to bear, but she still couldn't bring herself to ask.

She had been cold and wet and snowed on in New York. But there was always a doorway handy or a shop she could sidle into. Then suddenly she remembered standing with the matches in her hand outside A.T. Stewart's and the lady who smelled of lavender as she stepped from her coach and pressed a dime into Maggie's hand.

After that, Maggie had gone home to Ma, stopping on the way to buy a bun and some milk with her dime. She had climbed the broken, rickety stairs, filled with stench, and gone into the room they lived in with its rat holes and gaps in the plaster and the filthy ticking on the mattress and her mother, coughing her life out, clutching the nearest thing she had to a blanket. . . .

"Mag! Mag!"

She came out of the memory as though out

of a trance. Annie was tugging on her hand. "They've gone, Mag. I can't see the path — where do we go?"

The snow was coming thick and fast now.

Maggie was appalled at herself. "I didn't see her turn off," she said.

"She and Hannah just went. I don't think Hannah wanted to go like that, but Ellen was pulling her coat. Mag, where is the path?"

Maggie stared at the snow-covered flattened grass. Underneath there somewhere was the path Uncle James had told them to follow. Now, when she turned in any direction, everything was exactly the same. But it wasn't flat. If it were it would be easy to see the farm even at a distance. But she was beginning to understand there was a roll to the land hereabouts, and she knew the farm was below somewhere. But there was no telling where to go.

"Did you see which way they went, Annie?"

Annie put out an arm. "That way."

"Are you sure?"

"No. Oh, Mag, are we lost?"

"Of course not," Maggie said.

Annie came up and put her arms around Maggie. Maggie, who thought that Annie never showed signs of feeling cold felt her sister's small body shiver. "Are ye cold now?" she said.

And then, "I'll take my shawl for you."

She took her shawl off.

"But Mag, you'll get cold."

"What rubbish. I'm older and bigger. Now put this on. Do as I say!"

She was wrapping the shawl around Annie's shoulders when she thought she heard something. She looked up and there were Rufus and Rumpkin and behind them the wagon with Uncle James driving it.

"I thought you might have a little trouble after the snow started coming down so hard," he said. "Get up. Maggie, you take my coat."

"Oh, no — " But he was already wrapping it around her. Underneath he had on a wool shirt. "Now we'll be home before you can say Jack Robinson!"

"How was school?" Aunt Priscilla asked, when they were all in the cabin.

"Mary Prendergast has a cat named Chicago," Annie said.

"Fine," Maggie answered. "I brought this note for you from Miss Bailey."

Aunt Priscilla opened the note, read it and then put it back in her pocket. In a low voice she said to Maggie, "I think it will be fun to help you with the reader." She glanced up and searched Maggie's face. "What else happened?"

Maggie hesitated, then said, "I don't think Ellen McCandless likes me. She made some remarks about . . . about our being poor, and Miss Bailey made her sit in the front after that."

"It's the McCandless girls that James told you to come back with, isn't it? They live nearest us, so they'd be the obvious ones."

"Yes."

After a moment Aunt Priscilla said, "It's useless to say don't pay any attention to her, because I remember when people said that to me in a similar situation. Easy to say, hard to do. I'd speak to her mother, except that her mother . . . well, Ellen is like her. That plain child Hannah is worth ten of her, but I'm afraid nobody's ever going to know it."

She took a breath. "I was sewing on dresses for you and Annie today, using some flannel material I had left over from last year. Now let me fit it on you and see if it's right."

By this time Uncle James had gone back to the barn, taking Annie with him, so Maggie stripped off her old dress and stood in her shift while Aunt Priscilla, pins in her mouth, fitted the basic frame of the dress on her.

Suddenly Maggie said, "Have you cut out Annie's yet?"

"No. I thought I'd start with you. I think your dress is thinner than hers."

"She got cold today in the snow. I'd rather you'd do her first. If you don't mind." She added the latter as an afterthought.

"I believe I'll go on with this, Maggie, and then do Annie's. As I said, her old one is heavier. But I admire the way you always think of your little sister. You know, I share the responsibility with you now. You're both my daughters."

"Yes," Maggie said. She was busy thinking Aunt Priscilla was wrong and wasn't really listening.

The snow stopped later in the afternoon. Maggie had put on her boots and shawl to go out to the barn to collect any eggs the hens had laid, and to scatter some feed for them. They lived in a corner of the barn that had been fenced off, and it was part of Maggie's responsibility to feed them, take in the eggs and keep the area as clean as possible.

Annie was helping Uncle James with the afternoon milking. He had come in from the fields and was watching her as she pulled the teats on the large cow, causing a jet stream of milk to go into the bucket.

"Slow and easy," Uncle James said, standing behind her. He caught sight of Maggie. "Come and learn how to milk, Maggie. One of these days you may have to do it."

Maggie hesitated. She didn't like the great beast with its hot, manure smell and its wet lips. But she knew she had to learn, so she put the feed basket down and came over to where Annie was working on a stool.

"Get up, Annie. I want your sister to learn how to do this."

Obediently Annie got up. "You just pull down slow, Mag."

"I know what to do," she said.

But when she pulled on one of the teats as slowly and as firmly as she could the cow's head turned. The animal blew at her.

"Don't pinch her," Uncle James said.

Maggie tried again, trying to balance how much she pulled the teat with how tightly she held it. Hearing the beginning of a sound she leaped away from the stool. The cow's hoof missed her by an inch or two. The bucket of milk rocked a little.

"You don't have the hang of it," Uncle James said unnecessarily.

Maggie righted the stool and sat down. She was determined to milk properly and to get some milk. This time she didn't do too badly. Obviously the cow did not like it. And she was hampered by being poised to jump away at any moment. But she managed to get some of the milk into the pail.

"I think you ought to do that every day so

you can do it properly," Uncle James said. And then, in a louder voice, "Come on, kit kat!"

A thin orange streak went past Maggie.

"Put some milk in this," Uncle James said, and put a dish down beside the bucket. Maggie filled the dish with milk. The cat, walking back and forth, tail thrashing, waiting impatiently for Maggie to do this, plunged her nose into the fresh milk and lapped furiously.

"Ho ho," Uncle James said. "Look who's come for some!" A tiny black, orange and white cat wobbled in, looked around for a few seconds, then made its way to the dish. Putting its nose into the milk it sneezed, blowing milk in every direction. The orange cat looked up, aimed a slap at the kitten and then went back to drinking. This time the kitten approached the dish from the opposite side.

Maggie watched. Unlike Annie, she had no particular love of animals. Just watching over her mother and Annie had been more than she could handle. Animals were further trouble, ate food that people should have and were often dirty. Nevertheless, there was something about the doggedness of the little cat that appealed to her.

She sat there, watching her.

"Durndest thing," Uncle James said. "I drowned all the kittens, I thought, but I missed this one who wasn't with the others. Now I guess I'm going to have to drown her separate. We don't need two cats."

"No," Maggie heard herself say. "Please don't drown her."

Uncle James looked at her. "If you want her, she's yours. But you're going to have to do whatever looking after she needs. Aunt Priscilla and I don't have time to do any more than we are."

"All right," Maggie said.

Maggie fell into the school routine, making sure that her chores with Mrs. Vanderpool were done before she and Annie started out.

Uncle James took them to school in the wagon, but they came back by foot, slowly learning the way by recognizing landmarks — a tree stump, a sudden dip in the level of the ground, some trees in a clump across the white expanse. The snow stopped after the first evening, but, as Uncle James said, it would start again in earnest before too long. Often Spot would come out to meet them, each day coming farther from the farm, throwing himself on Annie with devotion and almost knocking her over. But she never feared him, and he would return with them, giving even Maggie a feeling of security. Maggie had not lost her fear of him, but she was grateful for his presence in this huge lonely country.

Ellen McCandless had returned to her proper seat in the schoolroom, and had managed to refrain from being deliberately rude to Maggie. Instead, she ignored her.

Maggie sat beside Tom, who teased her and secretly, when she was called on, helped her.

Aunt Priscilla now spent an hour each evening with Maggie, helping her learn how to read the reader. As she pointed out words and pronounced them, Maggie was able to pick them up quickly.

"You're doing well," Aunt Priscilla said during the second week. "Soon you'll be able to keep up with the others."

Maggie's dread was that somehow, before she really knew how to read properly, her failure would be betrayed, and she'd be publicly disgraced.

Since Miss Bailey never called on her for anything, except perhaps to recite a fact that had been given the previous day, she was protected. But one day, when they arrived at school, it was not Miss Bailey who was there, it was Mrs. Smiley, the woman from church with the hard, narrow mouth. She was taking Miss Bailey's place because their teacher was sick in bed. Only the best readers did well when she called on them.

"Who is she?" Maggie asked Tom under her breath.

"The widder of the man who used to be minister," Tom said. "She was teacher here before Miss Bailey. People say she's a terror. Sees sin everywhere."

"Why are you talking, Tom Brinton?" the high, scratchy voice suddenly snapped out. The substitute teacher rapped on her desk with her pointer. "Stand up, Tom, when I speak to you."

Tom rose to his feet. "Yes, ma'am."

"And now you can tell us what you were saying to the girl next to you. When I was young we didn't seat boys and girls together, and I don't approve of it. What were you telling her?"

Tom's cheeks flushed red, and there was a red saddle across his nose that Maggie had learned was a sign that he was angry. But he said calmly enough, "Just tellin' her that you were the widder of a minister we had, seein' as how she's too new to know."

"Is that one of the young 'uns from New York?" She peered shortsightedly at Maggie.

Maggie stood up. "Yes, ma'am." She felt that Tom shouldn't be punished alone.

"Think you're smart, don't you, coming from the East. All right. Turn to page one hundred and twenty-three in your reader and read from the beginning of the second paragraph."

Twelve

Maggie stared at the paragraph. She wondered if by some second sight the hard-faced woman standing at the front, a grim smile touching her slit of a mouth, knew that of all paragraphs in the reader, this one contained the most words Maggie didn't know.

"Well?" Mrs. Smiley said after a few minutes of silence. "Can't you even get the first word? I thought that anybody could do that."

There were one or two titters.

"The . . ." Maggie read, her face burning, her eyes trying frantically to unravel the mystery of the second word. There was a *p* and an *o* and an *i* —

"Anybody?" the teacher said.

Ellen stood up. "That's poinsettia, Mrs. Smiley. I thought everyone knew that."

"You would think so, wouldn't you? But maybe they don't know about poinsettias back East. Go on, Maggie. Now that somebody's told you that word, try the next."

Throughout the next twenty tortured minutes Maggie failed to read more than half the words of more than one syllable. As she stumbled and faltered, Mrs. Smiley's smile grew wider. Plainly she rejoiced at every humiliation, calling on various pupils to supply the missing answers, even, on one occasion, summoning a seven-year-old to show up Maggie's ignorance. Hardest of all for Maggie were the giggles at her mistakes. Some detached part of her knew that not everyone was laughing. But to her tormented pride it sounded like a wave of ridicule coming from everywhere.

"So all that fancy talk in the East is just that," Mrs. Smiley said, when Maggie stumbled to the end of her ordeal. "They can't read there any better than we can, can they, boys and girls?"

"No," shouted the assembled children.

"So maybe we won't be quite so uppity," Mrs. Smiley said.

Maggie stared down at the desk.

"Will we?" Mrs. Smiley persisted.

Maggie knew the teacher was expecting a "No, ma'am." But supplying it was beyond her.

She continued to stare down and remained silent.

"Just to make sure of that," Mrs. Smiley said, "I think I'll keep you in for a while after school, for some special instruction."

Maggie raised her head. "I have to get back," she said shortly. "I have chores I have to do."

"Oh? What things do you do that couldn't just as easily be done by your sister? You will stay here."

As Maggie's mouth opened, the woman snapped, "And don't you dare sass me!"

At the end of school that day, Mrs. Smiley said loudly. "Maggie, you will learn to read that paragraph. Open your book and start."

"I have to see my sister home," Maggie said.

"Oh, we'll be glad to take her as far as the fork," Ellen McCandless offered.

"No," Maggie said. "I must see her home."

"You will stay here and let Ellen and Hannah look after your sister. If you don't, I'll write a note to Mr. and Mrs. Russell, and you will not be able to come back to school again."

Maggie hesitated. It was true that she and Annie had learned the way home, even with snow covering everything. And for a week they had not even bothered to go with the Mc-Candlesses. In addition, the thought of re-maining ignorant while all these children were

163

continuing to learn at school was daunting. The Russells would be disappointed in her.

She turned to Ellen. "Please see to it that Annie gets off in the right direction," she said.

"I'm sure Ellen can be trusted to do that," Mrs. Smiley put in. "She's been here much longer than you."

"I'll be all right, Mag," Annie said.

So, reluctantly, Maggie saw the last of the children leave the schoolroom and turned to her reader.

Now that she was without an audience, Mrs. Smiley abandoned her sarcasm and simply drummed the difficult words into Maggie's head, making her repeat by rote vowels, consonants and syllables of the words she didn't know.

Determined to get out as soon as she could, Maggie did not argue with her, nor defend herself.

After what seemed a long time Mrs. Smiley said, "All right, you can stop now. But be prepared the next time I call on you. Others know their readers. I see no reason why you shouldn't."

The snow was falling when Maggie started home, and since there were no footprints left around the schoolhouse, she knew it must have been coming down for at least an hour.

But Annie should have been home by then, she told herself, answering a nagging voice that said she should have gone home with Annie, no matter what Mrs. Smiley ordered, instead of letting her pride concern itself with the Russells' possible disappointment.

As she stumped home, her boots sinking into fresh snow, she remembered something Ma had said. "Ach, Maggie, pride goes before a fall. Father O'Mara preached on that. It's going to get you nowhere, going around Miss High-and-Mighty."

She was struggling with the deepening snow when she finally stopped for a moment to remind herself of the landmarks: Going this way, due west, there was first the clump of trees far off to the right. Then, after the fork, there was the tree stump. She peered to her left, and it was then she realized that an early dusk had fallen and between the snow and the darkening sky she couldn't see twenty feet in front of her, let alone a clump of trees far off.

Fright skittered along her skin. Terror of the great emptiness, of the endless flat country, a terror that seemed always to be lurking near, closed in around her. She stood still, shivering, and remembered, marveling, that it was she who had wanted to come, who had forced Annie to take the train, to leave New York.

New York had been a monster, a filthy beast that threatened from every open doorway, filled with people who would steal the shoes from your feet if you dozed off for a moment.

But the horror that it had been was also familiar. The garbage-strewn streets, where pigs were loose to eat what they wanted, were filled with people — not emptiness. In the city she could close her eyes anywhere and know how to get home, even if home was a cold, squalid room. . . .

"Maggie! Maggie!" She heard the faint sound before she saw the lantern.

"Here!" she yelled. "Here!" And then she walked as fast as she could in the whirling snow.

She saw the heads of Rufus and Rumpkin before she saw Uncle James. He leaped down and was coming towards her.

"What in thunder happened? We've been waiting for an hour and a half."

"Didn't Annie tell you?" Maggie said, and knew, with a sick thud of fear what he was about to tell her.

"Annie? We haven't seen her. Where is she?"

"I'll have that woman up before the elders, so help me God, I will," Uncle James said, slapping the reins on the horses' backs. "Treating

166

you like that, and making you stay while Annie went home. I'm astonished the McCandless girls — " He stopped. "But I suppose I shouldn't be. Priscilla told me what had happened with Ellen. She's pretty as a picture but spoiled and selfish, just like her mother. But I sure never thought she'd let little Annie, who doesn't know the country, get lost. She could be buried in a snowdrift somewhere. I was in town, or I would have come sooner."

When they got to the McCandlesses' cabin Uncle James jumped down and knocked on the door. It was opened by a woman Maggie assumed must be Mrs. McCandless. Uncle James spoke for a moment. The woman peered into the falling snow, obviously trying to see Maggie. Then she turned around and said something. In a minute Ellen appeared. She hung her head while Uncle James talked. They were all joined by a man who came to the door just as he finished. He turned to Ellen.

Even though she couldn't hear what they were saying, it was obvious that Mr. McCandless was angrily reproving his daughter, who put her hands to her face.

In a moment Uncle James was back. "That worthless girl swore she saw Annie off on the right fork when they got to the divide. I don't believe her, and if it had been anybody but

Ellen I also think she would have gone with a seven-year-old child, seein' as it's snowing."

"Where can she be?" Maggie asked. Her mittened hands were clenched together.

"We'll go along the route home, calling out," Uncle James said. "Now you call as loud as you can, and so will I."

Maggie had no faith that Annie, wherever she was, would hear. But she called out as loud as she could, her twelve-year-old treble arrowing through the curtain of snow, then echoed by Uncle James's deep voice.

It was perhaps ten minutes later that Maggie, to her great shock, heard a faint, "Maggie! Maggie!"

She put her hand on Uncle James's arm. "Did you hear that?"

"No. Where?" He stopped the horses and let the reins lie still on their backs. Then he said, "Yes. I heard it. She must be under that bank where there's a hollow." And then, as another sound erupted, "Well, I'll be — "

Spot, heaving himself through the snow, was coming towards them barking frantically. Handing Maggie the reins, Uncle James jumped down and started pushing his feet through the fresh drifts down an almost invisible slope above a small stream. Maggie saw him reach down. When he straightened, he was holding Annie.

"Annie!" Maggie cried, and started to get down.

"Don't leave the horses," Uncle James called sharply.

In a minute he had put Annie in Maggie's lap. "Hold her tight," he said. "She's bitterly cold. Come on, Spot. Up!"

Maggie held Annie. "How do you feel?" she whispered. "Talk to me!"

"I'm cold." Annie's voice shivered with her shaking body.

Uncle James took the reins and urged the horses forward. Anxious to get back to the barn, they went as fast as they could.

Even so, Maggie asked, "Can't they go faster?"

"They're just as eager to get back as you are," Uncle James said. "No, they can't. Not through this."

"What happened?" Maggie asked Annie.

"I don't know. I just kept walking and it snowed harder than ever. Then I fell down. Then Spot came. He was warm, and I held him. Maggie, I'm so cold!"

"I think she'd be frozen without him," Uncle James said.

For the first time Maggie felt affection for the fierce dog. "Good Spot!" she said. And she felt his huge head push under her arm to lick Annie's hand.

"What happened to your mittens, Annie?" she asked.

Annie didn't answer.

"Keep her awake," Uncle James said. "We're nearly home."

Maggie shook Annie. "What happened to your mittens?"

"I dunno, Mag." She lapsed silent again, her eyes closed.

Maggie shook her. "Answer me!"

"They came off."

Suddenly, out of the murk, the cabin appeared. The door was open and light streamed out.

"James? Maggie? Are you there?" Aunt Priscilla called.

Uncle James let Maggie, Annie and Spot off at the door. Maggie had her arm around Annie, almost carrying her.

Aunt Priscilla came out and picked Annie up. "Help me get these wet things off her, Maggie," she said.

Quickly they stripped Annie, and Aunt Priscilla put her into a new flannel nightgown she'd made. Then she put her in bed under all the blankets they had, and the bed itself had been warmed with a warming pan. Then while Maggie held her, Aunt Priscilla fed her hot soup, putting it into her mouth, spoon by spoon. But Annie continued shivering until finally she drifted off to sleep.

Aunt Priscilla looked at Maggie. "You're wet, too, although not as much as Annie. Get out of your clothes. I've heated some water, and I want you to go behind the screen there and bathe with it and then put on fresh clothes."

When Maggie was finally warm and dry Aunt Priscilla said, "Now tell me, what happened?"

So Maggie told her about Mrs. Smiley and the paragraph and Annie supposedly going with the McCandlesses.

"They should have brought her back here, especially since it was snowing. But that Ellen wouldn't put herself out for anyone." Aunt Priscilla hesitated. "I suppose since you and James were there they're well aware of what happened. But I'll give Ellen's mother a piece of my mind when I next see her."

"Do you think Annie will be ill?"

"I hope not. Now get Mother's tray ready. I want to get her settled as early as we can this evening."

But Maggie had to go over the whole story again when she took Mrs. Vanderpool's tray in.

"Hmm," Mrs. Vanderpool said. "That Smiley woman is mean and vindictive. She doesn't like people from the East. She made that clear to me when she came here one day last summer."

"She thinks we're stuck-up." Maggie paused, then blurted out, "People always seem to hate people from somewhere else."

"Yes, well. . . . I told you I was sorry for what I said, Maggie. And I am. You're going to have to learn to forgive or you'll be miserable all your life, paying everybody back for old hurts. I should know."

They eyed one another, silently.

Then Mrs. Vanderpool said, "Do you like to read? I mean," she added hastily, "do you think you'd like to if you knew how?"

"Yes. I've always wanted to know how. I like stories. Ma used to tell us stories sometimes. I loved them."

"Well, I know Priscilla's helping you. But I'll help, too. You see that box over there?"

Maggie turned to see the chest in the corner. "Yes."

"It's filled with books. I get them out and read them when I can't sleep. You put some of those in your head and you can make the Smiley woman sing another tune."

Maggie was awakened while it was still dark by Annie, thrashing around in the bed beside her.

"What's the matter?" Maggie whispered.

But Annie kept turning, pulling the covers every which way, and muttering.

"What's that you're saying?" Maggie asked. Finally she put her feet on the floor, felt around for her candle, and lit it with the matches beside it. Then she held the candle over Annie and saw that the younger child's eyes were still closed as she muttered and twitched and thrashed.

Fear seized Maggie. She had seen that before with Ma, and knew it was the result of high fever.

"Annie," she said. "Annie! Wake up!" But it was no good. Annie's eyes remained closed, or if they did open, they were unfocused: She did not know where she was.

Then Maggie felt Annie's face and neck. They were burning hot, and when Maggie held the candle higher she could see Annie's cheeks were flushed.

Maggie got up, put her shawl around her, and dragged the cold water bucket over to the bed. Then she took one of the cloths from near the stove. She was trying to bathe Annie's forehead with cold water when the door at the other end of the room opened and Aunt Priscilla appeared, holding her candle.

She came over and watched Maggie for a moment. Then she said, "It would be easier if you got a pan and poured some of this water into it. Then we could use the water in the bucket for other things and wouldn't soil it. I'll take over here while you go and find a pan. Then you can put some water in the kettle and put it on the stove. And the fire needs building up with more chips. We mustn't let the room chill."

"It's all right," Maggie said brusquely. "I took care of Ma. I know what to do with Annie."

"What was the matter with your mother?"

"She had the sickness — consumption."

"I see. But I don't think that's what's the matter with Annie, and I believe I know how to cool her down now, without letting her get chilled. So please do as I say."

Maggie, wet cloth in hand, stared at Aunt Priscilla. "Ma told me to take care of Annie."

"Your mother told you also to come out here to find another home and another set of parents for you both. So, let me be the mother now. You've been the mother long enough for a girl your age."

Maggie might have dug in, if Annie hadn't at that moment opened her eyes and recognized her surroundings and the woman bending over her. "Aunt Priscilla," she said. "I'm hot."

"Yes, dear. I know you are. Now you just rest, and I'll try and cool you off a little."

Thirteen

Annie got sicker as her fever mounted higher. But Aunt Priscilla insisted that Maggie go about her chores as much as possible while she, Aunt Priscilla, stayed by Annie's bedside.

There wasn't much anyone could do besides bathing Annie's face with cold water and every now and then changing the sheets and her nightgown. This meant that in addition to her other work, Maggie had to wash the sheets in a huge tub filled with water heated on the stove and with soap that Aunt Priscilla had just freshly made. When the rinsing was done, Maggie was taught how best to hang the sheets on racks near the fire without cutting heat away from the rest of the room. After that, for hour after hour following school, Maggie would iron them. In addition, she also did Annie's milking and barn chores.

She would far rather have looked after Annie. But her protest was stilled one day when Annie called out, and Maggie was the only person in the cabin. Maggie stopped her ironing and went over to the bed. "What can I get you, Annie?"

Annie continued to thrash and turn.

Maggie, leaning over, asked her question again.

"I want Aunt Priscilla," Annie complained. Then she pushed Maggie away.

Aunt Priscilla entered the cabin at that moment. Maggie straightened. "She wants you, Aunt Priscilla," she said, and went back to the ironing on the table.

Uncle James harnessed up the horses and went into the town and brought back a doctor with him. Dr. Grew looked at Annie, put a wooden spatula down her throat, listened to her chest, and finally said to go on doing what Aunt Priscilla was doing — to keep her as comfortable as possible and as cool, without letting her get in any drafts, and to hope that the fever would break soon.

While they were waiting for the fever to break, Maggie was moved to a trundle bed in Mrs. Vanderpool's room. She fought the move.

"I want to be where I can help her."

Aunt Priscilla was sympathetic. "Maggie, I understand that, but I'm going to take your place, and I can do that better if I'm not worried about you, too." She hesitated. "We don't know what Annie has. The doctor doesn't recognize it. I don't know if it's catching, but I don't want to take a chance of your catching it."

So the trundle bed was put in Mrs. Vanderpool's room, and Maggie lay awake there instead of in the big bed beside Annie.

Mrs. Vanderpool snored, and she used the chamber pot at night with great frequency. Maggie hated being there.

One night two days after the doctor's visit, Mrs. Vanderpool suddenly spoke up in the dark. "You're not asleep, Maggie, are you?"

Maggie had been lying there, tense, waiting for Mrs. Vanderpool to start snoring.

"No," she said.

"Don't sleep a lot in here, do you?"

"No." Some sort of rudimentary politeness made Maggie say, "But I wouldn't sleep much out there, either."

She heard Mrs. Vanderpool moving around and the bed creaking. Then suddenly a match was struck and the candle lit. Maggie sat up in bed. Mrs. Vanderpool was slowly wrapping her shawl around her shoulders. Then she hobbled over to the corner, opened the box and took out a book. She got back in bed, placed the candle where the light would fall on her book, opened it and started reading aloud.

Maggie listened grudgingly. No one had ever read to her before. Ma was too busy working and too tired when she came home. Besides, Maggie was never entirely sure that she could read, because the subject was not discussed. And on the scattered occasions when Maggie went to school, the teacher or the nun either asked questions or wrote on the blackboard.

Then, as Maggie lay there in bed and Mrs. Vanderpool read aloud, the magic started to engulf her. She had never heard a book read like that before, or words like that. Some of them she didn't understand, but it didn't matter. Mrs. Vanderpool read well, and her rather crisp manner of speech, which had sometimes reminded Maggie unpleasantly of the ladies walking in and out of Stewart's in New York, made the words clear, like music. The story, in spots, was also funny, and Maggie laughed, although if asked she couldn't really have said why.

Finally Mrs. Vanderpool stopped reading. "Now," she said, "try and go to sleep." She blew out the candle.

The amazing thing was, Maggie went to sleep almost immediately.

When Maggie brought her tray in the following morning, she wanted to say something about how much she liked the book Mrs. Vanderpool had read. But she felt oddly shy. She had never said anything to Mrs. Vanderpool before in a kind or friendly way, and it was proving difficult. Finally, while Mrs. Vanderpool was buttering her corn bread, Maggie said suddenly, "What was that book? It was wonderful!"

"It's called *Alice's Adventures in Wonderland*, and it's by a man named Lewis Carroll." Mrs. Vanderpool looked at her sharply. "You liked it, did you?"

"Yes. It was — well, I never imagined anything like that! It's so silly, and yet it's so real."

"Perhaps we can read a little more tonight."

Annie's fever suddenly broke early one morning. She lay there, clear-eyed though weak.

When Maggie came home from school she went over to her and said, "I'm happy you're better. I was worried."

Annie gave a feeble grin. "Mag, do you think you could let Spot in? It'd be grand to see him. And he saved my life."

"Do you remember being in the snowdrift? I asked you before but you couldn't think back."

"I remember being frightened and cold and

179

then sleepy and knowing I was lost. I remember Spot finding me. I hugged him, and he was warm. I dreamed about him, coming for me."

Maggie was aware of hurt and disappointment. "So he's driven out Timmie?" She knew she shouldn't have said that, but she couldn't stop herself. It wasn't Timmie that was left out. She, Maggie, was.

"Ah no, Mag. You know I'd never forget Timmie. But Spot likes me."

Maggie went out to the barn to ask Uncle James about Spot.

"It's true," he said. "She wouldn't be alive today if it weren't for him. Yes, you can take Spot in, but come back. There's the milking and the chickens."

So Maggie ran across the snowy yard with Spot lolloping after her. When she opened the door, Spot hurled himself in and onto Annie's bed. Then Maggie went back to the barn.

After a while she noticed that the tiny kitten Uncle James had given her was watching her while she milked. So she filled the saucer and waited for the mother cat to turn up.

But the mother cat didn't come, and the little kitten had a hard time with the milk, plunging its face in, then choking and spitting out as much as it had taken in.

"Where's the mother cat?" Maggie asked Uncle James.

"She went out — silly cat! God knows why. Maybe the mice here were all frozen. Anyway, she got caught by something, maybe a coyote. There wasn't much left of her. Pity. She was a good mouser."

"So there's none left but this kitten."

"That's right. But its eyes are barely open, and it's too young to survive by itself."

"What'll happen?"

He shrugged. "It'll die, or I'll have to drown it."

"Can't you do anything?"

"Yes, if I had the time, I could make a teat out of a small piece of cloth and let it suck on that, dipping it in milk. But I don't have the time." He stuck his fork in some hay. "Why don't you do it?"

The kitten chose that moment to wobble up and rub itself against Maggie's leg as she sat on the stool. It was scrawny and so young its ears almost didn't show, but it had a loud voice and seemed to be pleading for some kind of attention.

"Show me about the teat," she said to Uncle James.

He got a cloth from the tool shelf, made the corner into a small spiral then dipped it into the milk. "Hold the cat on your lap," he said.

Maggie picked up the cat and put it in her lap. Then she watched as Uncle James lowered the pointy teat into the kitten's mouth. It latched on and started to suck the milk. After a moment, Maggie took it out, and with the kitten protesting, dipped it again into the milk and put it in the kitten's mouth. After a while it had drunk quite plentifully and settled down to sleep in some straw.

"Are you going to give it a name?" Uncle James asked.

"I don't know," Maggie said. "I hadn't thought." But then she remembered the cat named Chicago. "Yes, I'll call it New York."

Annie got slowly better as the weather outside got colder. More snow fell. It was part of Maggie's job to bring in buckets of chips each day from the barn, along with her other duties of setting the table, washing and drying the dishes, milking the cow, feeding the chickens and keeping their area clean, taking Mrs. Vanderpool's trays in and out and helping her bathe each morning. She also helped once a week with washing and drying and ironing the clothes.

All this was done before and after school. Each morning Uncle James hitched up Rufus and Rumpkin and took her there and, in the coldest weather, picked her up, although when the sky was clear and the wind didn't blow too hard she came home with Ellen and Hannah McCandless to the fork where they turned off. They didn't talk much, although one day when Ellen was kept at home, Maggie found Hannah likable and interesting.

Miss Bailey was back in school. Once, when Ellen made some giggly comment about twelve-year-olds who couldn't read, Miss Bailey asked her quite pleasantly if she would like to come to the front of the class and recite the multiplication table. When Ellen muttered, "No," Miss Bailey asked if anyone else would like to.

Maggie put up her hand. She and Miss Bailey had gone over the multiplication table during lunchtime the previous day. It was something Maggie found quite easy to learn, especially when it was taught in a little jingle.

She got up and vindicated herself by being word and number perfect. "Perhaps," Miss Bailey said, "you'd help Ellen with her arithmetic if she needs it."

Maggie had never told Miss Bailey about that terrible morning when Mrs. Smiley had been there, but she knew that Miss Bailey knew. For all the great distances and more limited chances of meeting, news and gossip, Maggie found, traveled as quickly in Kansas as they did in New York, especially when most of the people in the community and at school attended the same church.

Spot stayed more and more in the house with Annie, and less and less in the barn. Uncle James grumbled about his being softened up, but his presence kept Annie cheerful and entertained and took some of the pressure off Aunt Priscilla.

Every night, after they had both gone to bed, Mrs. Vanderpool would open *Alice's Adventures in Wonderland* and read aloud. Maggie looked forward to that more than to anything else during the day. For an hour or so, the loneliness and the fear of the huge dark outside and the sense of being trapped among foreigners would recede behind the adventures of Alice and the March Hare and the Mad Hatter.

She never mentioned the reading aloud to anyone, not even to Miss Bailey. She was quite sure Aunt Priscilla and Uncle James could not remain ignorant of the voice reading aloud albeit in another room at the other end of the cabin. But it was never referred to, and while she and Mrs. Vanderpool would discuss the book when they were alone, she never mentioned it to anyone else.

She also didn't really notice that she herself

was spending more and more time with Mrs. Vanderpool, under such pretexts as combing the older woman's hair and helping her put it up, or bringing a new quilt to put on her bed.

And Annie went on playing with Spot and talking to Aunt Priscilla and being coaxed each day to eat a little more of the milk and cornmeal mush and the beans and the occasional chicken soup that Aunt Priscilla urged on her.

One day, more than two weeks after Annie's fever had broken, Maggie was listening to her prattle and realized, with a sense of shock that Annie now talked a little like the Kansans. R's sounded in her words more, and her vowels were growing stretched and flattened. And she hadn't mentioned Timmie or Mrs. O'Gorman since long before her fever broke. She now talked more to Aunt Priscilla than to Maggie.

Maggie kept her sense of exclusion in hand. What she had of her very own was the hour that Mrs. Vanderpool read to her, bringing alive things she'd never dreamed of.

Then one day when Maggie came home she found Mrs. Vanderpool sitting by Annie's bed, her stick propped against her chair, reading aloud. Annie was lying back against the pillows listening with shining eyes.

Maggie stood there in the door until Mrs. Vanderpool rather sharply told her to shut it.

"Some of us are cold," she said. "And your sister is just getting over an illness."

"How was school today?" Aunt Priscilla asked.

"All right."

Maggie picked up a bucket and went out to the well that lay between the cabin and the barn. By the time she had brought the water back, and put some of it in the kettle on the fire, she had pushed to the back of her mind her jolt at seeing Mrs. Vanderpool reading aloud to Annie.

But that night, when Maggie saw Mrs. Vanderpool getting out *Alice's Adventures in Wonderland*, she said, "You don't have to read to me if you don't feel like it. You must be tired."

Mrs. Vanderpool stopped moving around. "Don't you want to be read to tonight? Are you tired of *Alice*?"

"It's just that what with reading to Annie and all — "

"As you wish." Mrs. Vanderpool blew out the candle and lay down in bed again. "I thought you liked it."

When Maggie brought her tray in the following morning, Mrs. Vanderpool snapped at her that the coffee was not hot enough. "Take it back and pour me some that hasn't been standing in a cold room."

Maggie took it back to the main room, then tripped on the foot of one of the clothes racks that had been pushed to one side. The coffee spilled over some of the clothes and the floor and the cup broke.

Uncle James and Aunt Priscilla were sitting at the table having breakfast. Outside, the first full light of the day was driving the clouds up into the sky.

"Watch out for those cups," Uncle James said. "They come from my mother, and they're the only ones of the kind we have."

"Butterfingers," Annie said from the bed.

Aunt Priscilla got up. "I'll take her some more coffee, Maggie. You finish your breakfast in peace."

Uncle James cleared his throat. "We brought Maggie here to — "

"Live with us and be our daughter," Aunt Priscilla finished. "Which she is doing. Daughters sometimes drop things. So do sons. Didn't you, when you were a little boy?"

Uncle James got up and went out to the barn. Maggie ignored Aunt Priscilla's suggestion about finishing her breakfast, and started to clear the table.

"Mag, can I have some more milk?"

"I'm sure Aunt Priscilla will be glad to give you some. I have to get ready for school."

"You're gettin' mean, Mag."

Maggie swung around. "I am not. But you're gettin' to be like all the people here. You're not like us anymore."

"But t'was you wanted us to come, Mag."

Aunt Priscilla came out of Mrs. Vanderpool's room, shutting the door. She looked, Maggie thought, rather strained.

"Can I have some more milk, Aunt Priscilla?" Annie asked.

"Maggie'll get it for you."

"No she won't. I asked."

Maggie went over to the pitcher, poured some of the milk into a cup and took it over to Annie. What she wanted to do was box Annie's ears, but she knew that she was wrong even feeling such a thing, let alone wanting to carry it out. What would Ma have said?

There came into her mind words her mother once had spoken to her: "It's the green-eyed monster, Mag. You're going to have to be watching it. Your da was jealous. He was jealous about everything. He once nearly knocked a man down because he had spoken to me. And all he was telling me about was the price of some eggs cheaper than those Mrs. Mulroney was sellin'. But your da had some notion in his head that this man had a likin' for me back in Ireland when we were young. It was terrible."

While Annie was talking, Aunt Priscilla had glanced at Maggie in a worried way, started to say something and then stopped.

"You'd better start to school, Maggie," she said. "It's getting late."

That night when Uncle James was in the barn and Aunt Priscilla was in talking to Mrs. Vanderpool, Annie said suddenly, "I saw Ma, Maggie."

Maggie whirled around. "What are you talking about?"

"About seeing Ma. When I was sick. I saw her clear as anything, sitting with the Blessed Virgin. She said they were both watching over us."

"It was a dream!" Maggie almost shouted.

Tears filled Annie's blue eyes. "Mag, it was real. I know it was real."

Fourteen

Annie finally got well enough to get out of bed and dress and be around the cabin, but Aunt Priscilla kept her home for the next few weeks.

Maggie moved back into the main room of the cabin and resumed sharing the bed with Annie. Since the night she had refused Mrs. Vanderpool's offer of reading aloud she had heard no more of *Alice's Adventures in Wonderland*. She missed it terribly. And since they had discussed the book so much when Maggie was helping Mrs. Vanderpool with her trays and her bathing and her getting dressed, not discussing it made big holes of silence in the times they were together.

Whenever she thought of it, which was every time she was in Mrs. Vanderpool's room, Maggie struggled to devise some way she could, casually, introduce the subject of *Alice*. But the right words in the right tone never seemed to come. And she'd let the morning or evening pass without mentioning it. Then at night she would lie awake beside Annie, wishing that she were in Mrs. Vanderpool's room and Mrs. Vanderpool was reading *Alice* aloud.

Always then she would decide that the next morning she'd say something about it to Mrs. Vanderpool. But in the morning another voice — which was still her own — would jeer in her head: "She'd just refuse if you did ask. And then you'd have humbled yourself for nothing." Humbling herself was something she associated with Ma's having to be nice and polite to the rich ladies who ordered her around and said rude things about the Irish and accused Ma of stealing when she took home some food that had been left over.

It was a daily battle. She wished with all her heart that Mrs. Vanderpool would bring it up herself, or that Aunt Priscilla would.

But no one said anything.

The kitten, New York, grew rapidly, and graduated to lapping milk for herself and sharpening her little claws in Maggie's boots.

Maggie and Annie now had two new dresses

each, one of linsey-woolsey and one of calico. And Maggie wore on her head to school a modified sunbonnet in a dark brown.

In arithmetic, geography, and history she was rapidly catching up with the others, but her reading, though better than before, was still halting, and every time Miss Bailey started calling on the children to read aloud from the reader, Maggie was filled with dread of what she was convinced would be her humiliation.

So far Miss Bailey had managed not to call on her, but Ellen could never resist a dig during lunch- or playtime afterwards. "And when are you going to read to us, Maggie?" she'd tease, and would burst into giggles, along with one or two of her admirers.

When that happened, Tom would try to stick up for Maggie. Once he said, "And when are you going to honor us with the multiplication table, Ellen?"

Ellen tossed her head. "Girls aren't supposed to know arithmetic, Tom Brinton." Then she lowered her lids with their long lashes. "Would you like me if I recited the multiplication table?"

He turned red. To say no would be to run the risk of being punished for rudeness to a girl, because, with his two younger siblings at school, his mother would hear about it within five minutes of his getting home. "I'd like you better if you weren't so mean," he said.

"I'm sure your ladyfriend would never be mean, even if she can't read!" Followed by more giggles.

When the weather was good, and as though nothing had happened, Maggie and Ellen and Hannah would then go home together as far as the fork. Maggie was too frightened of getting lost again to risk going on her own, especially since the snow was now more than a foot deep and still occasionally falling, and each day the landscape looked different. Maggie never enjoyed those walks. She felt that Ellen had the upper hand and that she knew it. As before, on the rare occasions when Ellen was not at school, Maggie went home with Hannah. They talked about a whole variety of things, and Maggie enjoyed it immensely.

Aunt Priscilla had not yet resumed Maggie's reading lessons, because taking care of Annie who was at home all day had absorbed the little extra time she had formerly given to teaching Maggie.

Then one day when Maggie took in Mrs. Vanderpool's breakfast tray she found the old lady lying flat in her bed, wheezing and fighting for breath.

Frightened, Maggie ran out to Aunt Priscilla, who dropped everything, ran into the room, took one look, and went into action. First she told Maggie to bring all the pillows from all the beds. These she propped under her mother's head, and when they didn't seem enough, she and Maggie folded the quilt off of Maggie's and Annie's bed and stuck that behind also. This made Mrs. Vanderpool's breathing easier. After that, Aunt Priscilla ordered Maggie to put some water on the stove, and then go out to the barn and ask Uncle James to harness up Rufus and Rumpkin and go into the town to get the doctor.

Maggie didn't go to school that day. Instead, in addition to her own chores she did those that were usually Aunt Priscilla's. She cleaned the cabin, washed the dishes, collected the ingredients for a thick, nourishing stew, rolled out some cornmeal, chopped some of the vegetables from the ones Aunt Priscilla had preserved, made the beds, milked the cow, fed the chickens, and did some of the clothes wash that Aunt Priscilla usually did that day. In addition, she brought from the barn an extra bucket of buffalo chips for the stove.

Annie trotted around after her, helped her dry the dishes, helped with the beds, but was forbidden to go out to the barn because a high prairie wind was blowing.

"Please, can Spot come in?" Annie asked.

"Yes, all right, when I come back from the barn I'll bring him."

The doctor came and went into Mrs. Vanderpool's bedroom. When he came out he said to Maggie, "I'm so glad Mrs. Russell has you to help her. Her mother's had a heart seizure and is going to need a lot of attention and nursing, and I hope you can save her some of the extra trouble, because she isn't that strong, herself, and doesn't need any more on her."

"Yes," Maggie said. "I will."

She wondered if Uncle James had asked the doctor to say that when he was driving the doctor to the house. While the doctor was speaking to her, Uncle James was standing by the fire, staring down at it. But she knew he heard everything, and she remembered then the times he had interrupted his wife to tell Maggie to do something instead of Aunt Priscilla's doing it because that was why they had adopted her and Annie.

Maggie stayed home from school then and kept house while Aunt Priscilla was in with her mother, bathing her forehead, giving her medicine, helping her when she was suddenly sick to her stomach or hit with intestinal cramps. It was Maggie who took out the commodes and emptied them and provided fresh clean ones. She washed and ironed sheets so they could be ready for Aunt Priscilla to change them, which she often had to, and helped in making the bed so as to disturb Mrs. Vander-pool as little as possible.

Annie was given chores of her own, and Maggie took to letting Spot in almost all the time, because when Annie wasn't busy, she'd be happy playing with Spot, or stroking him, whereas if she were alone Maggie would be hard pressed to find something to keep her out of the way.

Then, one afternoon as she was helping Aunt Priscilla with the bed, she noticed how thin Aunt Priscilla had grown, and how the lines in her face had deepened.

Uncle James did not talk much at dinner. He, too, looked strained, and it was obvious that Aunt Priscilla was too tired to make much of an effort. Once she said, looking across the little table at Maggie and Annie, "This is not a cheery time for you both. I'm sorry."

"But this is why we adopted Maggie and Annie," Uncle James said rather harshly. "I wanted them to help you with the work. For times like this. If they can't spare you, there'd be no point in having them."

It was his tone even more than the words, Maggie thought, that was upsetting. Annie's eyes filled with tears. "Don't you want us now?" she asked.

"Of course we do, Annie dear," Aunt Priscilla said. "We love you and Maggie."

Uncle James got up, put on his cap and jacket, and stamped out.

"Men often get upset by illness," Aunt Priscilla said. "And he's very fond of Mother."

"Will . . . will she be all right?"

"We hope so very much. But she's weak and needs all the attention I can give her, which is why I am so grateful to you, Maggie. You're a great help."

And then Aunt Priscilla got ill. It started with a bad cough that got deeper and deeper. A flush appeared in her cheeks.

Uncle James, coming in one night and seeing his wife bent over the table for a moment, her hand on her side, ordered her to bed.

"I can't, James. Mother still needs nursing."

"Then let Maggie do it. But you're going to bed." He turned to Maggie. To her he seemed angry. "You're going to have to look after them both. I'll try and get some help for you from the neighbors."

In a way, the nursing was the least of her burdens. She had spent so many months look-

197

ing after Ma that she moved instinctively between boiling water, sponging Aunt Priscilla's
forehead, trying to get Mrs. Vanderpool to
drink some of the soup she had prepared, and
emptying the commodes. Uncle James helped
when he could with lifting the women and
changing the beds.

Then one day a wagon drove up and depos-
ited a Mrs. Sinclair. She was an elderly woman,
probably around Mrs. Vanderpool's age, but
strong and full of drive. She was living with
her son and daughter-in-law some miles away
and had offered to come and help.

She was, indeed, a help, but Maggie was
more worn out when Mrs. Sinclair's son
called for her at night than Maggie had been
when she was alone. Mrs. Sinclair was bossy.
She did not approve of a great number of
things that included the way Aunt Priscilla
usually made her soup, the dust over much
that was in the cabin, people from the East,
the Church of Rome and the presence of Spot.
About all of these she expressed herself in
short, condemnatory statements, except for
the presence of Spot. She simply ordered him
out.

Annie started to cry.

She whirled on the child. "I will not put up
with spoiled children. Animals are filthy crea-

tures of no use except when they are needed by human beings."

Annie cried even harder, and then started to cough.

"Take this cloth and dust every single thing in this room," Mrs. Sinclair said. "If I hear any more out of you, I'll take a slipper to you."

Maggie turned. "You'll not lay a hand on Annie."

"And who is going to stop me? You?"

Luckily Uncle James came into the cabin at that moment. "No one," he said, as he took off his cap and outer jacket, "takes a slipper to anyone in this house."

"Spare the rod — "

"It's my house. And in my house my orders are obeyed."

Maggie threw him a grateful look, but when Mrs. Sinclair had left he said, "I don't know what went on with Mrs. Sinclair before I came in. You have a sharp tongue, Maggie, and from what I hear you're not backward about using it. I'll not have you insulting the women who come to help us. We need them. You need them. So in future please hold your tongue."

Mrs. Sinclair did not come back. Mrs. Johnson, a much younger, gentler woman turned

199

up two days later, having been driven over by her husband. They had just moved into a cabin and were even newer on the prairie than Maggie and Annie.

She was a great help, and Maggie enjoyed her presence. But after the first day Mrs. Johnson couldn't return because her own child had come down with a cold, and she didn't want to take any infection back to him.

But others came and from them Maggie learned that theirs was not the only household with more than half the members incapacitated.

"I'd a been here sooner," Mrs. Marshall said, bustling about the cabin, "but I was helpin' Amy Barton. Silas Barton's real sick, and she's got two of her three young 'uns flat on their backs. And the McCreadys are down, too — all six of 'em, not one up to bring in water or make soup." She glanced at Maggie. "You'll learn winter can be a hard time here — especially after the first big snow."

Mrs. Marshall and the other women who came cooked and cleaned while Maggie was busy nursing Mrs. Vanderpool and Aunt Priscilla. Some of them were bossy and Maggie sensed their disapproval of the East and most things different from themselves. But they were also kind and helpful and matter-of-fact.

And more than anything else this touched Maggie's heart. Neighbors in New York did not do this. Perhaps, Maggie thought, it was because among the Irish things were so desperate they could hardly help themselves, let alone anyone else. Of course the rich, grand ladies went around being charitable, but that was different. Here, people helped one another.

Sometimes, when Maggie went out to get water or to empty slops she caught herself looking in a new way at the snow-covered miles around. Somehow, knowing that the people she couldn't even see would come to help, made a difference in how she saw the endless prairie. It was not anymore the great emptiness.

Maggie kept hoping that Uncle James would say something about how well she was doing with the nursing. But he said nothing. And one night at dinner when Annie asked if Spot could come in again, he snapped at her that animals in the West were kept to work, not as lapdogs.

Annie started to cry. Uncle James sprang up with a sound and went into the bedroom where Aunt Priscilla lay.

"It's Aunt Priscilla," Maggie said to Annie. "She's that sick." And if she died, Maggie thought, what would happen to her and Annie?

A while later Maggie, going into Aunt Priscilla's bedroom carrying hot water and a bowl of soup on a tray saw the big man sitting on the bed, holding his wife's hand, tears coming silently down his face.

She paused. "Uncle James?" she said timidly.

Without looking at her, he got up, face averted, and left the room.

That night in bed, Maggie felt Annie shaking, and knew she was crying. She turned and put her arms around her sister.

"Is Aunt Priscilla going to die like Ma?" Annie said.

"I don't know," Maggie answered.

There was silence for a while.

"Will they send us back, Maggie?"

"I don't know," Maggie said again. "If they do, you can see Mrs. O'Gorman and Timmie."

"Yes, but I like Spot, and when Uncle James isn't cross with me I like being here."

She should have remembered, Maggie thought, that Annie was only seven. She loved easily, but she forgot easily, too.

Back in New York, she thought, along with Timmie and Mrs. O'Gorman, they would also see Mary and the other children who walked the streets and slept in doorways.

In that moment Maggie knew how much, despite the loneliness and people like Mrs. Smiley and Ellen McCandless, she wanted to stay.

Fifteen

Mrs. Vanderpool started getting better. Her breathing was easier and some of the gray look had left her face. But as Maggie trotted in and out of her room and brought her water and food and helped her move around in the bed, Mrs. Vanderpool said almost nothing. Maggie didn't know whether it was because the old lady was still having trouble breathing and was trying to save her breath or because of the strain that had been between them.

Then one day she asked, "How is my daughter?"

"She's . . . she's getting better," Maggie said. The lie felt bitter on her tongue.

Mrs. Vanderpool stared at Maggie. "You're a poor liar, I'll say that for you."

The doctor came the next day.

"Well, Mrs. V.," Maggie heard him say, as he was about to leave Mrs. Vanderpool's room, "I think you're going to weather the attack this time."

"How's Priscilla?"

The doctor hesitated. Finally he said, "We should know pretty soon."

Mrs. Vanderpool spoke with sudden passion. "She should never have come out here! And neither should I! She was always frail, and it's too hard a life for her."

"Isn't that why you took in those orphans from New York?"

"Much good that's done!"

"That's not what I heard," the doctor said. "The neighbors say the older one's willing and hardworking."

"Yes, and proud as a peacock!"

"You mean she won't let you boss her around."

There was a silence. Then Maggie heard Mrs. Vanderpool's voice. "I ought to know about pride. I have more than enough of it myself. But I wish . . . Oh, well." Then, "I wish I could help Priscilla more."

"Just say a prayer for her. That's all any of us can do."

A new neighbor arrived soon after and helped Maggie with cooking and nursing. The snow and wind had stopped, so Annie, well bundled up, was allowed to go to the barn to help Uncle James.

Later in the afternoon the neighbor's husband, who had been in town, drove by for his wife, so Maggie was left alone in the cabin.

She was standing in the middle of the main room, one chore finished, the next not quite begun, when she thought she heard a noise coming from the Russells' bedroom.

Knowing that she was alone, terrified of what she might find, she stood for a moment, frozen. Then she ran in.

Aunt Priscilla lay as she had lain for the past ten days, eyes closed. For a moment Maggie thought that she had stopped breathing. Maggie was no stranger to death. She had seen it on the ship coming over, and even though she was only six at the time, she had not forgotten the sight of the greenish, sunken faces. She went quickly over to the bed.

"Oh, God, Holy Mother, please don't let her die. Please!"

Leaning down, she took Aunt Priscilla's hand. "Don't die," she whispered. "Please don't die! If you die we'll have to go back."

She had squeezed tight her eyes. When she opened them Aunt Priscilla was looking at her. "I won't die, Maggie," she whispered. "I promise you." Then she gave a tired smile.

Maggie put her face down beside Aunt Priscilla's and, for the first time since she had been in Kansas, cried.

After a minute Aunt Priscilla's hand came up and lay against her cheek. "It'll be all right," she said. "You'll see."

Everything seemed to be lighter and easier after that. Aunt Priscilla's strength returned slowly but steadily. She ate the soups and stews that Maggie prepared with apparent relish.

"You're getting to be a really good cook, Maggie," she said one evening after dinner when Maggie came in for the tray. "Isn't she, James?"

Uncle James smiled. "She is." He hesitated. "As a matter of fact, we couldn't have managed without her these past few weeks."

When she and Annie were washing and drying the dishes later he came out and said, "I meant it back there, what I said. I know I've been, well, severe. I was worried about Priscilla."

Quickly, and to Maggie's surprise, he put an arm each around the two of them and kissed each on the cheek. "No daughters born to us could have done more."

It was a week later when Maggie, having collected Mrs. Vanderpool's dinner tray, suddenly heard herself say, "Would you read to me tonight?"

Mrs. Vanderpool looked at her. "Why don't you read to me?"

Maggie flushed. "You know I can't read well."

"Yes you can. You start, and I'll help."

"I don't have my reader here. It's at school."

"I didn't say anything about a reader. Don't like most of them, anyway. Too full of good people doing good things. Get *Alice* out of the box over there. You can start where we left off. When you don't know a word I'll tell you what it is."

So they went on with *Alice*. Whether she had improved more than she realized, or because she forgot herself in Alice's adventures, or because Mrs. Vanderpool turned out to be a born teacher, Maggie didn't know. But she found she had less and less trouble reading. It was also great fun going back to discussing Alice and her friends off and on during the day.

The following week Maggie and Annie returned to school. This time Spot went with them, and sat in the warm schoolroom sleeping while they did their lessons.

In a clear voice Miss Bailey asked how Mrs. Russell and Mrs. Vanderpool were doing. Everyone stopped talking. Miss Bailey waited until they were quiet, then went on, "I have heard from several people how helpful you were, and how Mr. Russell couldn't have managed without you."

Annie grinned. Maggie's cheeks grew pink with pleasure.

Miss Bailey seemed to hesitate, then she said, "Of course, we have gone on with the reader in your absence. But now that Thanksgiving is near, do you think you could read to us the story about the pilgrims that's on page one hundred and forty-eight?"

Maggie found the page and stood up. Her heart beat fast. For a moment the words blurred. Then they cleared. Maggie saw that she could read the first sentence perfectly well. And then the second. And the third.

She could read!

Feeling that suddenly whole worlds were opening up around her, she sat down, flushed and happy and thinking about all the books in Mrs. Vanderpool's chest.

"That was great," Tom whispered.

Maggie smiled at him. "Thank you." And then, "It felt good."

Turning back, she encountered Ellen's sullen gaze. Maggie gave her a big grin and had the satisfaction of seeing Ellen turn away.

Thanksgiving was celebrated in the church in the morning and with a dinner in the church hall immediately afterwards. Everyone went. Even Mrs. Vanderpool with her walking stick was bundled up and put in a special part of the wagon that had been prepared for her.

Maggie had helped cook the turkey and make the pumpkin pie. Annie had stirred the mincemeat. When the preacher said grace before they ate, he thanked the Lord for a whole list of blessings and ended with a special thanks for the arrival in their community of two such wonderful, hardworking children as Maggie and Annie.

When he said that Aunt Priscilla, who was sitting between them, took a hand of each and squeezed them. Uncle James, who was sitting across from them and next to Mrs. Vanderpool, smiled. Maggie was astounded to see Mrs. Vanderpool wink. After a minute she winked back.

It was while she was helping clear that Maggie looked out and saw Annie, who was outside piling up snow into some kind of shape, not high, but long. "I wonder what she's making," Maggie said aloud.

Aunt Priscilla, who was beside her, glanced out. Then she looked at Maggie. "Why don't you go out and help her?"

Maggie hesitated. "The dishes — "

"You can come back and do them. Now run along. You haven't had much time for fun."

Maggie paused, then put down the dish she was drying and dried her hands. Running out she said, "What're you making?"

"Spot," Annie said.

"It doesn't look like a dog," one of the other children said. "It's like a cabin."

"I haven't finished," Annie protested. Under her quick hands what looked like a muzzle and neck emerged. Then she bent and scraped away at the bottom, hollowing out and pulling away the snow so that the body and what could be legs began to emerge.

Maggie scraped long with her. The snow was cold through her mittens, but she was warm from the big rich dinner and their efforts.

"Here," Dr. Prendergast said, coming out of the churchhouse. He had been watching Annie from the porch and had brought two berries with him from the kitchen, which he now placed on either side of the muzzle. "Those are his eyes."

"And this is his collar," Tom Brinton said. He wrapped a discarded ribbon from one of the

211

cakes around the snow-dog's throat.

When they were through, the snow pile looked more or less like a dog-shaped creature who could be Spot.

"There now," Maggie said, and laughed. "It looks just like Spot." Impulsively she hugged Annie. Then she ran back to finish helping in the kitchen.

When she was carrying the clean dishes to put in the hampers, she suddenly found herself confronted by Mrs. Smiley.

"Heard you're becomin' a right good reader," she said.

Maggie stiffened a little. "I love reading."

"How do you like Kansas now?"

For a moment her mother's face flashed across her mind, giving her pain. Then Maggie took a breath. "I like it a lot," she said. "It's home."

About the Author

ISABELLE HOLLAND is the author of more than forty books, but she admits to being particularly attached to Maggie and Annie of *The Journey Home*. The daughter of a foreign service officer, Ms. Holland was born in Basel, Switzerland, and grew up around the world, spending many years in Guatemala and England.

Ms. Holland is presently living in New York City with her four rascally cats.

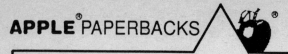

APPLE® PAPERBACKS

Pick an Apple and Polish Off Some Great Reading!

BEST-SELLING APPLE TITLES

❏ MT43944-8	**Afternoon of the Elves**	Janet Taylor Lisle	$2.75
❏ MT43109-9	**Boys Are Yucko**	Anna Grossnickle Hines	$2.95
❏ MT43473-X	**The Broccoli Tapes**	Jan Slepian	$2.95
❏ MT40961-1	**Chocolate Covered Ants**	Stephen Manes	$2.95
❏ MT45436-6	**Cousins**	Virginia Hamilton	$2.95
❏ MT44036-5	**George Washington's Socks**	Elvira Woodruff	$2.95
❏ MT45244-4	**Ghost Cadet**	Elaine Marie Alphin	$2.95
❏ MT44351-8	**Help! I'm a Prisoner in the Library**	Eth Clifford	$2.95
❏ MT43618-X	**Me and Katie (The Pest)**	Ann M. Martin	$2.95
❏ MT43030-0	**Shoebag**	Mary James	$2.95
❏ MT46075-7	**Sixth Grade Secrets**	Louis Sachar	$2.95
❏ MT42882-9	**Sixth Grade Sleepover**	Eve Bunting	$2.95
❏ MT41732-0	**Too Many Murphys**	Colleen O'Shaughnessy McKenna	$2.95

Available wherever you buy books, or use this order form.

Scholastic Inc., P.O. Box 7502, 2931 East McCarty Street, Jefferson City, MO 65102

Please send me the books I have checked above. I am enclosing $_____ (please add $2.00 to cover shipping and handling). Send check or money order — no cash or C.O.D.s please.

Name_____ Birthdate_____

Address _____

City_____ State/Zip _____

Please allow four to six weeks for delivery. Offer good in the U.S.A. only. Sorry, mail orders are not available to residents of Canada. Prices subject to change.

APP693